MW00577419

khulud khamis is a Palestinian writer and activist, born to a Slovak mother and a Palestinian father. She holds a Master's degree in English Literature from the University of Haifa and works in the field of social change. She is a member of the feminist organization Isha L'Isha – Haifa Feminist Center. She lives in Haifa with her daughter. This is her first novel. khulud publishes some of her writings on her blog at: <www.HaifaFieldnotes.blogspot.com>.

# *Haifa Fragments*

## khulud khamis

SPINIFEX

First published by Spinifex Press, 2015

Spinifex Press Pty Ltd
504 Queensberry Street
North Melbourne, Victoria 3051
Australia
women@spinifexpress.com.au
www.spinifexpress.com.au

Editors: Bernadette Green and Susan Hawthorne
Copy editor: Maree Hawken
Cover design: Deb Snibson
Typesetting: Claire Warren
Typeset in Stone
Printed by McPherson's Printing Group
Cover photograph Estelle Disch, 'Structure', 2013. Reproduced with permission.

National Library of Australia
Cataloguing-in-Publication data:
khamis, khulud, 1975–  author.
Haifa Fragments / khulud khamis
9781742199009 (paperback)
9781742198972 (ebook: epub)
9781742198958 (ebook: pdf)
9781742198965 (ebook: kindle)

*For my parents, Emilia and Nassim*

# Acknowledgements

I would like to thank my parents, Emilia and Nassim, for being patient and supportive throughout the whole process of writing this novel. My daughter, Michelle, for putting up with my moods during the writing process. I owe a large part of my development as a writer to the community of Isha L'Isha – Haifa Feminist Center's women. I found in you sisters, friends, and mothers. You gave me the strength and courage to bring my writing to a completely new level, and to realize that my voice has legitimacy to be out there in the public sphere, and not only in my desk drawer. Special thanks to my two dear friends Galia and Talma who have always been there for me, picking me up during difficult times, guiding, supporting, and motivating me. To Naief, thank you for your love, your endless support, and for making me laugh.

I would like to express my deep gratitude to Susan Hawthorne from Spinifex Press for believing in me and for seeing the potential of my manuscript, and for giving me this invaluable opportunity to publish my work. Last but not least, I would like to thank my editor, Bernadette Green, for her sensitivity, understanding, and gentle yet professional handling of my text. I couldn't have asked for a better home for my first novel than Spinifex Press.

When Maisoon was sixteen, her grandmother called her into the salu.[1] Shifting her ample frame on the old sofa she made room for her granddaughter. She cupped Maisoon's face in her hands and her granddaughter's dark hair fell over her arms. "Maisoon, I want to tell you the story of your name." She patted Maisoon on the knee and didn't stop until she had finished.

"It was 1948, Haifa's last battle. I was eight months pregnant. Seedo was away with the rest of the young men. I don't know what he did exactly, because he refused to carry a weapon. The Yahud lived up the mountain, and we were down here. The night the first barrels were rolled down from Share'a El-Jabal ... I remember that night. I was alone at the house with your father Majid. I heard screaming outside, and I saw our neighbour Haneen running out—and up and up the mountain.

"She had six small children in the house. Her husband had been among the first ones to be killed, and she lost her mind. Haneen the majnouny we called her. She would wail for hours every night. It was like the sound of an animal. I don't think she ever slept. Someone from the church had come and tried to take her children. Ya rab! I never saw a mother fight like Haneen for her children. Haneen's whole world was her family ... On that night, she wanted to stop the barrels with her bare body. When I saw her running, I didn't think. I took little Majid in my arms and ran after her, but Haneen was fast and I was pregnant. Or maybe I should have left Majid at home but I couldn't ... how could I ...

---

1. A Glossary appears on pp. 169–173.

"That night a woman from the church came and took all of Haneen's children. And that night I lay down on the kitchen floor and bled. I bled and I looked up and I saw through the window that the sky was red. There were sparks flying, I thought is there a celebration, someone getting married? How could they at this time ... or is the sky bleeding Haneen's death. I didn't understand. I thought I must be losing too much blood to see the sky sparkling like that.

"Seedo came back in the morning. I thought his clothes had my blood on them but it was not my blood. I asked Abu Majid what happened and he only looked at me and my bloody clothes and lay down next to me and we wept. The next morning the woman from the church came back and told us there was a ship taking refugees to Lubnan and we could go with Haneen's six children. Your grandfather told her to go away, we had already lost one and we would not leave our home. I held on to little Majid so tight that he started screaming. Seedo buried the little one in the garden. I couldn't bear leaving her there all alone so we couldn't go away because of her.

"When Majid was fifteen I told him about that night and he asked me if she had a name. I told him I named her Maisoon. He gave her back to me when you were born but he made me promise never to tell you so you don't carry her history, his history, our history in your name ... But I don't have the right to take this with me to the grave. Majid will understand one day."

# 1

ا The alarm clock went off at 3:45. Maisoon fumbled in the dark, brushing her arm on something warm and hairy. Yamma! She forgot Ziyad was spending the night. Again. She scrambled out of bed, turned on the bedside lamp, and stole a look at him. He looked so unruffled when he slept, nothing like the waking Ziyad, full of unspent energy. Butterflies could have flown in and made a bed in different parts of his body. A lingering scent of their love-making, mingled with the remains of cheap red wine filled the room. I can't go to the checkpoint smelling like this.

"Where you going, habibti? It's the middle of the night." Ziyad's voice was a hoarse whisper.

Maisoon stopped dead in her tracks. It was Saturday, so any excuse would be flimsy. She decided to tell him the truth and deal with it later. "I'm going with Tamar to the checkpoint to pick up little Ahmad. He's got an appointment at the hospital this morning." She immediately headed to the kitchen, turning on the water heater on her way.

Maisoon loved her dilapidated kitchen with its falling-apart wood cabinets—the kind they don't make any more. A window overlooked the souk. It would soon come to life, with vegetable and fruit vendors setting up their stalls, greeting each other Assalamu Alaikum and Sabah el-kheir. The strong, bitter smell of kahwa with cardamom would soon permeate the souk, penetrating the thin, uneven cracks between the stones.

Maisoon's apartment was located on the second floor of an old building in the middle of Wadi Nisnas souk, right above Um Muhammad's stall.

"Mais?" Ziyad's voice echoed from the bedroom, "Do you seriously have to go? Min shan Allah, it's Saturday! It's my only day off and I wanted us to spend it together. Can't someone else pick up this kid and drive him to the hospital?"

"No," Maisoon's reply came flat from the kitchen. She walked over to the bedroom and took a deep breath. "The schedule was made last week and I signed up for today's morning shift. People are counting on me." As an afterthought, she added, "This is important to me, Ziyad. And the kid has a name. It's Ahmad." Without waiting for a reply, she went back to the kitchen to make a cup of kahwa for herself.

Half an hour later, Maisoon was snuggled up in a warm blanket in the back seat of Tamar's car, sipping her kahwa. She looked over the steam at Tamar. Her age was hard to pick although she had no visible lines on her face, her curly hair was more white than black. "I don't get you, Tamar. You've been doing this for what—almost twenty years now? Where do you get the strength to go on?" Maisoon admired Tamar, no matter how impossible the situation she always came up with a solution. She was tiny, but when she needed to she could look imposing—even the soldiers at the checkpoints went out of their way to make sure everything went smoothly when Tamar was around.

"I just wake up every morning knowing I have no other choice," she said, glancing at Maisoon from the rear-view mirror. "So, how's Ziyad?" They were heading east, driving through the green of Marj Ibn Amer Valley.

Maisoon kept her gaze on the distant hills, "He's fine ... I guess," she sighed.

"He's fine. You guess. You've been with him for over two years now, ya binti, and you guess he's fine?"

The Arabic words sounded a bit off coming from Tamar, although Maisoon had heard her speak Arabic on numerous occasions. "There's

2

no wedding any time soon, Tamar, if that's what you're getting at. I'm not ready to give up my freedom ... yet."

"Is it because he's Muslim you think you'll have to give up your freedom? Well, let me tell you. I've been around for quite some time and living in a Muslim village for the past six years. In case you haven't noticed yet, Mais, they've abandoned their tents and camels. And they even own refrigerators!" A smirk was forming on Tamar's face.

"Oh Tamar, please! Stop making fun of me! It's just that ..." Maisoon's voice faded; she was careful to veil her thoughts.

The rest of the journey to the checkpoint passed in comfortable silence. For several months now, Maisoon would join Tamar on her Machsom Watch early morning shifts. Tamar's regular partner was going through chemotherapy and often couldn't make it. They were doing well with long silences. Tamar would drive and Maisoon would either watch the scenery or steal some sleep.

حيفا فراجمنتس

At around one in the afternoon, Ziyad heard Maisoon's voice float up and through the bedroom window.

"Assalamu Alaikum, ammi Abu Nidal ... no, thank you, I'm tired and if I drink your kahwa now my heart would start racing. I really need to get some rest." Her voice sounded drained and the feet shuffling upstairs were not a good sign.

Not again, Ziyad thought. The bastards probably didn't let the kid in. He braced himself, forcing a smile as Maisoon walked in with several small bags: homemade olive-oil soap, spices, kahwa with cardamom, bottles of olive oil.

"Salam. You still here?" she said as she slid into the armchair in the salu, closed her eyes, sinking deeper into the chair. "We waited for three hours at the checkpoint. Three hours, Ziyad. They kept telling us that he had the wrong permit."

Ziyad was standing by the window, studying Um Tawfiq hanging

3

laundry on her balkon. Um Tawfiq always took her time to hang the laundry, making sure all the clothes were meticulously lined up, the socks all facing the same direction, hanging according to colour. Tiny soldiers: white socks with deep blue stripes exercising to the gentle rhythm of the wind. On the line opposite, some brown socks danced to that same rhythm. "What do you mean, the wrong kind of permit?" he asked.

"I don't know, Ziyad. They just wouldn't let him in. Tamar tried all of her contacts, but it didn't work this time. I think the soldier at the post was a fresh one. Probably not familiar with the drill. They're supposed to let the kids in, Ziyad! Everything was set up, we had the confirmation letter from the Israeli doctors and the official letter from the hospital. But they just wouldn't listen. They wouldn't even look at the papers we had."

Ziyad hated these moments. He felt distanced from it all. It was happening in a different world. He came to her and kneeled beside her, stroking her cheek. "You know, maybe next week. Maybe they'll let him in next week."

"Maybe?" Maisoon looked at him in astonishment. Is that all he could say? But she was too tired to get angry. All her rage had been spent at the checkpoint.

"You know the saddest thing, Ziyad? I could see little Ahmad on the other side of the fence. The whole time—three hours—he was just looking at our side of the world. At first you could see his eyes filled with hope, he even smiled at me. But as the time passed, and he saw Tamar screaming into her mobile, his hopes began to evaporate. When we finally got into the car to go back, he didn't look disappointed. It was something much worse. I think he lost his faith in the goodness of people today ... and he's just a little boy, Ziyad."

Ziyad tried to detach himself from little Ahmad. "Your father called while you were out. I know, I shouldn't have answered, but who thought he'd call after ... anyway, I think he was just as surprised to hear my voice as I was to hear his."

4

Maisoon sat upright. Her father had kept his distance for over four months, ever since she announced that her 'partner' was from Ar'ara, the heart of the Muslim Triangle.

"He loves you ... you know."

"Oh, he does ...? So you're on his side now?" Maisoon's voice was flat.

"I'm not on anybody's side, Mais, min shan Allah. I just think his reaction was reasonable. That's how things are. This is how it's been for ages. You can't expect him to change his beliefs—the values he grew up on—just because you decided you're going to be with a Muslim man. It doesn't work that way."

"What do you mean that way? It works that way for me!"

"Ya Rab, Mais! We've been through this so many times, why can't you just let it go?"

"Let go of what?" Maisoon's voice was beginning to falter, trembling like the crystals of sugar stirred in her morning kahwa. She didn't want to repeat the words said so many times in so many ways. So she let it go.

Getting up from her chair, she walked to the kitchen, feeling relieved at the sight of the dirty dishes piled up in the sink. It was one of her small triumphs. Defying the mould Ziyad wanted her to fit into. And her father. And Um Tawfiq. She opened the fridge, hesitating. Hummus and labani with some of the olive oil she'd brought from the checkpoint. "Ziyad, could you go down to Abu Adel and get some bread?"

While he was gone, Maisoon took her time washing the dishes. The simple, cyclical repetitions allowed her mind to drain. While she concentrated on the movements of her hands, thoughts of her activism, her father, Ziyad—were all forced into a corner of her brain.

When Ziyad came back, they ate in silence, her fingers cautiously avoiding his while dipping her bread in the labani. Ziyad stayed in the apartment for another hour, reading on the diwan. When he saw that her silence would last the day, he gathered his things, gave her a hug, and left. She didn't resist—not when he hugged her, and not when he turned to leave. It was their way of staying together.

# 2

ك Colourful dresses and scarves were strewn all over the diwan when Ziyad came in with fresh grapes from Um Muhammad's stall. Maisoon didn't want to go to the henna party but she'd given in to her mother's insistence. She finally settled on a long, light blue sleeveless dress with a pattern of small yellow flowers, a cleavage that wouldn't insult anyone's honour and a deep, rumman-stained scarf.

Not knowing anyone except the bride and her parents, Maisoon settled in a corner of the garden, smoking a cigarette and sipping her wine when a young woman approached her. She was tall and slender, her features blurred in the darkness.

"I wish I could smoke a cigarette like you do … you know … in front of everybody," her voice was soft with a slight tremor.

"Ya salam," Maisoon laughed "and why can't you? Here, why don't you have one?"

The girl shrank back. "Are you majnouny? What would they say about me?"

Maisoon shrugged her shoulders. "So how about some wine, then?"

"Hmmm …"

There was something unfamiliar about the way the words danced on the girl's tongue—an accent Maisoon didn't recognize. "Maisoon," she said as the girl sat down on the stone next to her, brushing Maisoon's sleeveless arm as she took the glass of wine from her.

"I'm Shahd," and she giggled into the glass.

"And does Shahd go to school? What, tenth grade, eleventh?" Maisoon was losing interest in the girl.

"Actually, I'm twenty-three. I want to study medicine and become a daktora. Inshallah next year."

Maisoon was looking intently at her now. The girl was defining herself according to the norms of society—by age and occupation or education. She didn't look more than sixteen or seventeen with her slim body and virtually flat chest.

"Come, let's dance!" In a sudden movement, Shahd grabbed Maisoon's hand and dragged her to the middle of the garden, into the reflected lights. "It's one of my favourites!" She took her scarf and wrapped it around Maisoon's voluptuous hips. "Yalla ya amar, show us some of that hazz sharki." Shahd was now laughing, swaying her arms and getting down on one knee the way men do.

Maisoon's body froze, now what? Should she just do the elegant moves, dancing the way 'good' girls are supposed to? She looked down at the young woman whose name meant honey and allowed her body to decide. Closing her eyes, she let the music surge through her—dum-tak-tak dum-tak. Dum-tak-tak dum-tak. Deeper now and into her bones. Ach, to hell with all the women's talk. She checked the scarf around her waist, making sure it was tied at the right height. When Maisoon opened her eyes, she no longer saw the women sprinkled around the garden, nor did she see the mother of the bride staring at her in horror. It was only her, Shahd, the music, and the wine spreading warmly inside her body. There were no men at the henna, so she felt at ease to let herself be led by the rhythm completely.

She was lost in her own world of the durbakki and didn't see the way Shahd's eyes were transfixed on her, hungrily devouring every movement of her hips. She wasn't aware of Shahd's slight shiver of the body.

By the end of the evening, Maisoon was spent. The women who at first had looked at her as if she were committing a sacrilege were all over her by the time the music faded.

"Ya salam! Mashallah, you dance like an Egyptian!"

"No, didn't you see the way she moved her feet? That was Iraqi rakes. Where did you learn to dance this way?"

"Come to my daughter's henna next month and dance for us!"

"My son is finishing his law degree this summer, he's a very good boy. Come to our house for shai."

It took Maisoon a while to wriggle out of the grip of the women. She found Shahd in that same unlit corner of the garden where they first encountered each other. She was smoking one of Maisoon's cigarettes, abandoned when dragged to dance. "Hey, you! This was all your fault! And anyway, you're not supposed to be smoking in front of them."

Shahd didn't look at Maisoon—instead, she stared at her own bare feet. Her sandals were somewhere around. "I don't know … I lost track of time and Mansour is already gone to the hajez." Her eyes reflected a mix of uncertainty and fear, "Mama will worry about me, and Baba … and my ta'ashira was only for the day …"

The words hajez and ta'ashira hung in the air. That's why I couldn't place the accent. Maisoon dropped next to her, and reached for the burning cigarette. "Tayyeb, I live nearby, why don't you come for some hot shai with na'ana and we'll work something out."

Shahd straightened her back and looked at Maisoon. "Thanks for the cigarette." Then, very slowly, her face lightened. "Yalla, what are we waiting for? Shai sounds just like what I need right now."

حيفا فراجمنتس

"Watch your step," warns Maisoon, though she knows the words to be useless; the street is dimly lit. She hears Shahd recalling Allah in whispers as her sandals squash something decomposing, one of the less delightful parts about living in the middle of the souk. The night air smells of rotten vegetables mingling with the odour of fish. "It's not far from here, come."

Twenty minutes later, they are settled on Maisoon's old diwan, sipping shai with na'ana. Shahd has managed to call her neighbours and ask them to deliver a message to her family letting them know that she'll be staying in 'the city' tonight, not daring to mention the word Haifa, as the mukhabarat were probably on the line.

Shahd flicks through an old album of traditional Palestinian dresses, while Maisoon sketches her.

"You have beautiful hair," Maisoon says absentmindedly, "I've never seen such a colour." Shahd's long shiny hair is the colour of black olives. Her eyes a deep brown, almost black, are sprinkled with violet dots that dance when she laughs.

"Are you a painter?"

"Oh, you mean the sketch? No, no, it's nothing really. Just something to do with my hands, you know, like smoking ... I'm almost finished, but it's not good. I couldn't catch the light in your hair." She passes the drawing to Shahd.

It's almost midnight, but neither of them feels like going to sleep. When Shahd asks, "How come your parents let you live on your own?" Maisoon doesn't sense any judgment.

"Well, I am a grown-up woman. I didn't want to stay at home with my parents and wait until I got married, especially as I'm not planning on getting married any time soon," she pauses, then adds "or ever."

The teacup in Shahd's hand quivers. She doesn't know if the 'or ever' is said as a sign, or if Maisoon is one of those 'free, independent' women who don't believe in marriage. Or if she is doing this just to spite her parents. Or, maybe ... but this is a dangerous space which she can't yet explore. A space which demands careful navigation. There are moulds already made for her; their clearly defined boundaries are not to be crossed under any circumstances. For those who do—the price is always too high to pay. But this woman here, Maisoon ... she lives on her own, breaking taboos herself. But you've only known her a few hours. And she dances like a goddess. Oh and that body—so full of sensuality ... stop it.

9

Maisoon finishes her tea, disappears into the kitchen, and returns with a bottle of red wine, no glasses. "Here, open this while I change into something more comfortable. I've been saving this for a special occasion."

Shahd has never opened a bottle of wine before, but she doesn't need to be a daktora to figure it out. After several attempts she succeeds. Maisoon emerges from the bedroom wearing a men's old gallabiyya, hiding all those lush curves.

Maisoon holds the bottle to her mouth and tips her head back, Shahd studies her neck, one, two, three gulps and it's passed to her. Shahd balances the bottle between her legs as she lights her third cigarette.

"So, why did you invite me over? I mean, you don't even know me, and you could get into trouble for having me at your place. I could have asked the parents of the bride to stay at their house."

"Tfaddali, my home is your home. But seriously, you just looked really desperate and I wanted to help."

They finish off the bottle, laughing into the night, laughing at the shock and horror on the old women's faces when Maisoon began to dance. Their conversations are disconnected threads coloured with wine. It's almost dawn when they finally fall asleep on the diwan.

حيفا فراجمنتس

The following morning Maisoon calls Ziyad to see if she can borrow his car.

"Why borrow? I can take you anywhere you want to go."

"I need to get to Tal E-Zeitun to take a friend home. And I might be late."

Ziyad has never heard of Tal E-Zeitun. When she tells him it is in the West Bank, the line goes silent for a few moments. He knows better than to argue with her. "I'll bring the car in an hour, but I'm not going there with you." He doesn't want anything to do with the other side of his world.

It is well into the afternoon when they finally leave Haifa behind. Shahd is adamant that they shouldn't go through the checkpoint; she is sure they'd use her expired ta'ashira to put her in administrative detention. Maisoon doesn't know which is more dangerous: facing the soldiers or going through the no-go area.

"Look, see that small mound with the olive grove? There's a dirt road we can take."

This is just unreal … it's not happening to me, is all Maisoon's brain is capable of coming up with.

"Don't worry, it will be fine, Inshallah. I've done this before."

Ten minutes later, they are on the other side of the olive grove—on the other side of the green line. Maisoon is in a daze.

During the forty minutes it takes them to reach Tal E-Zeitun, the reality begins sinking in. I'm not welcome in this part of the world. I'm not one of them. I'm a citizen of the state that occupies their land. I have a blue ID in my wallet. I'm a traitor. I have running water and I don't need to worry that my home could be demolished at any moment, or that soldiers could raid my house in ungodly hours of the night. What am I doing here, putting myself in danger. If the mukhabarat find out, I'm the one who'll be spending the night in jail.

Maisoon pushes aside the immediate implications of her crossing the border and tries to focus on Shahd's family and how they'll welcome her. It is not her first time in the West Bank; but it is the first time she is going to the home of a Palestinian family living on the other side— so close yet worlds apart. Will they accuse me of betraying our people? Our land?

"Hey, you're thinking too much," Shahd says as they enter the mukhayyam, the refugee camp. "Look, there's Sami, my little brother. You can just pull up here and park on the side of the road. It's difficult to drive inside the camp; the streets are too narrow and you might run over one of the kids playing in the street."

Um Loai welcomes them with warmth. She hugs Maisoon tightly

and thanks her in so many poetic words for bringing her daughter home safely.

Settling down in their narrow salu, Maisoon's anxiety melts away with the heat. Um Loai serves lunch on a big silver platter; mhammar and bamiah.

"It tastes just like my mother's cooking, yislam ideeki, khalti," Maisoon says in between bites.

Um Loai smiles, "Of course it tastes just like your mother's cooking, habibti."

After some kahwa sada, Shahd takes Maisoon for a walk through the camp. They meet the neighbours along the way, Maisoon expects some hostility once Shahd tells them she's from Haifa, Aruset El-Bahar, but she receives nothing but warmth. Until now, her only encounters with Palestinians from the other side have been sporadic and distanced —mainly communicating with them through the fence at checkpoints or at olive harvests she has occasionally taken part in. But all those past encounters were never on equal ground. She was the privileged one coming to help the helpless. Walking through the camp with Shahd, she slowly relaxes and soon feels comfortable, her ears taking in the untainted form of the ancient language of this land.

When they return to the family house, Shahd's father is home. Abu Loai is polite but Maisoon can see that his smile is forced. He is in his mid-fifties, has strong arms and huge hands.

"Ahlan wasahlan, ya binti. This house is your house." His words sound sincere. "Um Loai here tells me you're from Haifa? I used to work in Haifa, in construction. You know, before they closed us up in these cages like untamed animals. Back then, we could at least make a living with dignity. But now ..." he looks down at his hands. His voice is empty of anger, his eyes dimmed with resignation, his hands reading uselessness.

Um Loai walks in with shai just as Maisoon is getting ready to leave. "It's getting late, binti. You can't go back home, the checkpoint will be closing and you don't know your way around."

12

Maisoon hadn't thought of any logistics until now. She doesn't even know how to get back to the checkpoint. She feels trapped but she has no alternative. She thanks Um Loai for her kindness and dials Ziyad's number but can't get through. There is no signal.

The small salu is turned into a bedroom at night, shared by Shahd and her two younger sisters, Ina'am and Shirin. Maisoon feels guilty when Shahd tells her sisters they have to share a mattress, but the girls just giggle and ask for a story.

"Kan ya ma kan, but not so long ago, there was a young girl who lived in a small small place. The place had just one gate from which you could come and go, and the gate would only open for half an hour in the morning and half an hour in the evening. But to leave the place, you had to have a special magic card. Now this girl lost her card ... then she found a secret passageway ..."

The girls fall asleep midway into the story, and Shahd motions Maisoon to follow her outside. "I want to show you something very special."

They walk through the dark, narrow alleyways. Small clusters of young men stand in doorways and on corners talking and laughing. Older men play shesh besh and smoke nargila. Here and there veiled women stand in twos and threes, talking in hushed voices. They pass a man in his sixties, sitting in the doorway of one of the haphazardly built two-storey houses. Even in the dark Maisoon can tell there is something wrong with him; his eyes follow her with an unsettling hollowness. Shahd tells her that Abu Fayyad lost his mind after his son exploded himself on a bus in Haifa back in 2003. Maisoon shivers and crosses her arms.

Near the edge of the camp, music streams toward them from a compound made up of three buildings. Small lights—red, green, white—run their length, creating a feeling of celebration. Patches of colours—paintings done in children's strokes, butterflies, flowers, animals—decorate one wall, while another reflects political resistance art—mainly Handalas, hands tearing at a wall, symbols of freedom.

13

Across one wall, Maisoon can read in beautiful Arabic calligraphy Dar El Amal. House of Hope.

"This way," Shahd takes Maisoon by the arm, leading her to one of the buildings.

Inside, they are greeted by a young man busily sweeping the floors. "Salam, Shahd. Oh! We have a visitor?"

"Masa'a el-kheir Qais. This is Maisoon, from Haifa. She's stuck here for the night." Shahd winks at Qais, who smiles back at her. "I don't know why they keep you, Qais. Really, I've never seen such a sloppy cleaning job." She quickly ducks to avoid the broom.

Maisoon watches them and wonders if Qais's smile is more than brotherly warmth.

They walk through a corridor with colourful drawings tacked to the walls, passing closed doors. The compound has three examination rooms in all, a spacious reception room, and two offices for the doctors. After the clinic, they go inside the second building—the kindergarten. Shahd tells her that it only opened a few months ago, and they are still getting organized. The third building will serve as an open house, with a big hall and several large rooms. They are setting up a library and a computer lab, and are planning an art room. The hall serves as a place for the teenagers to spend time together instead of roaming the streets.

Later as they are lying in bed, Maisoon asks about Qais.

"His family is rich. One of the richest in the Triangle," Shahd rolls over to face Maisoon. "The whole family went to England in the 1980s. Qais told me that his father didn't want the children to grow up as second-class citizens. Even though they had a comfortable life in exile, they wanted their children to remain connected to the motherland. So Qais spent every summer here. He fell in love with Palestine and when he was still in medical school, the idea of a clinic began to form in his mind." Ina'am mumbles something in her sleep, Shahd waits a moment before continuing in a whisper. "His father told him to speak to the sheikh of their community in exile. They raised enough money to open a clinic. Salaries and accommodation weren't an issue, as a number of

14

young Palestinian doctors and medical students were i
internships, and local families offered up their crammed
to host them.

"The clinic has been open for almost a year now. A...
sure Qais is there from seven in the morning until after ten at night, six
days a week. He has a diwan in his office and tries to catch some sleep
when he can but I don't think that's too often. He's so bright ... and his
heart belongs here." Shahd whispered into the darkness. "That's where
I work. Qais knows I want to become daktora."

حيفا فراجمنتس

Ziyad was cooking a shakshooka in Maisoon's apartment when she
came home the following afternoon. "You didn't come home last
night," he said without looking up from the pan.

"And you stayed in my apartment," she walked toward him and
hugged him, resting her head on his back. His body was stiff. He turned
around and held her tight in his arms. Too tight ...

"Go and take a shower, Maisoon. I'll make us some shai, we need
to talk."

As Maisoon rubbed the loofah over her body, any desire to share
her experience of Tal E-Zeitun with Ziyad was scrubbed away.

"You can't act like this, disappearing for two days. Without letting
me know you won't be coming home, turning your phone off. And
with my car, too!"

They were sitting on separate diwans, Maisoon's toes reaching Ziyad's
thighs. He was massaging her feet using too much pressure. She closed
her eyes. It was a one-way monologue. So she settled for replying to
him in her mind. You don't own me, you don't own me, you don't own
me. I can turn off my phone and disappear for two days. Tayyeb, maybe
not with your car, but I can do what I like. You don't own me, Ziyad.

15

**3**

When she woke up, daylight was slithering away from the souk, making space for the lazy hue of the evening. Ziyad was gone. She reached to feel the spot where he had been sitting; it was still warm.

She quickly ran down the stairs to catch Abu Nidal's last finjan of kahwa, still wearing her gallabiyya, having to hold it up so she wouldn't stumble. She heard some children laughing from one of the balkons.

"Look, look, like what old men wear in film Misri! Walla!"

An involuntary laugh escaped her; she stopped, looked up and did some dabka steps for the kids. They jumped up and down, delighted with their reward. Majnouny all the way.

Back in her apartment, she settled on the diwan with her sketchbook. Need something exquisite here for the Yahudiyya. She went through her most recent sketches, the ones inspired by traditional Palestinian dresses. No, she'd probably want something abstract and modern. Not anything that would remind her of a history she'd rather delete.

She had practically stumbled upon Giveret Amalia a couple of weeks before in Hadar, when she was on her way to meet Ziyad. She was texting him and bumped into the elderly lady. The lady looked at her in scorn and mumbled something under her breath. Maisoon apologized and was about to walk off when the lady caught her arm a bit too forcefully.

"Wait," she said, her face softening just a fraction. "Where did you get that necklace?"

Maisoon's hand went up to her neck, she felt the cool stone on her fingers. "I made it, I'm a jewellery designer."

The lady studied Maisoon's dark face, connecting it to her accent. She thought for a moment, then took out a card from her shoulder bag. "Here, call me at this number tomorrow morning at nine thirty." She turned around and walked away, leaving Maisoon standing there with the card in her hand, people swishing around her. *Amalia's Jewellery*.

On the phone the following day, Amalia skipped small-talk and asked Maisoon to bring some sample pieces of her work to her boutique. She didn't go into any details about business; once they'd arranged a time she hung up. Maisoon was thankful that she'd been smart enough to schedule their meeting for the following Friday, which gave her just enough time to put together a sample that was representative of her work without compromising her style.

She leafed through the sketchbook but couldn't focus. The images were moving around on the pages. The rings looked like snails and the bracelets took the form of knotted olive tree trunks. She moved to her worktable, pushing everything into a heap on the side—Ziyad was always complaining about the chaos, how can you work in such disorder?—and spread the velvet roll on the surface. She scanned the earrings and necklaces. Light blue and red beads. Translucent grey and purple stones. The yellow light that licked the jewellery made her squint.

She was still moving the pieces around in no particular order when her mobile rang—it was Shahd. Since the two nights they'd shared— one on this side of the world and the second on the other—they were on the phone at least once a day.

"Salam from the mukhayyam, habibti!" Shahd's voice came through fresh and spicy. "Mansour is taking some men through on Tuesday night and asked if I wanted to breathe for a couple of days. Is your diwan still on offer? I'd have to spend the night."

"Let me think about it," Maisoon teased, "hmmm ... yup, I think it should be available. But not for free." She looked at the roll of jewellery, "You'll have to pay your stay by helping me figure out the pieces for the Yahudiyya."

حيفا فراجمنتس

The following morning, Maisoon was woken by the clanking of crates being stacked on top of one another, in preparation for the big Eid. She took her kahwa to the narrow balkon and sat on a wicker chair, savouring the smell of the souk in the morning as much as she despised it in the evening. Wafts of fresh fruit—guava, saber, teen—swirled around her, carried by the gentle naseem. In these moments, she understood why people stayed on in the Wad, refusing to move on. It was the comfort in knowing that Um Muhammad would be there the next day with her fresh vegetables, that Abu Nidal would always have kahwa on the little coffee table ready for anybody who cared to sit with him and talk, that Um Tawfiq's laundry would be fluttering in the naseem on her balkon. Nothing would be changing any time soon. No new stones would be put in place of the old.

She finished her kahwa and went inside to choose the right outfit for today's meeting. She didn't want to look too Arab but neither did she want to look like she was trying to shed her identity. She felt a burden descending on her as she recalled the awkward moments of non-recognition, "What's the accent?" then the confusion, "I'm from here, born in Haifa," and finally, the silence of embarrassment, "I'm an Arab." Sometimes the reaction would be an embarrassed smile, or an, "Oh, you don't look like an Arab," or that all too common, "I have a very good Arab friend, Ahmad, maybe you know him? He's got a heart of gold, and I'm not just saying it, oh and he's the best car mechanic," or some such version of it.

She settled on a pair of blue jeans and a plain white t-shirt. Sandals and a blue scarf tied on her bag in case she got cold in the air-

18

conditioned boutique. No. Not the blue scarf. Not in this place where every colour was weighed down with history and meaning. Her favourite ones were forbidden to her: the black-and-white kafiyyah her father had given her. Long ago it lost its meaning; politicized when the West turned it into a symbol of terrorism, and then again de-politicized when it started being mass-manufactured by brand labels in all colours of the rainbow. In winter, she would put her kafiyyah on, wrapping it around her shoulders, and stand in front of the mirror. Then, with a thread of sadness take it off and hang it back, leaving part of her identity at home. This time it was the colour of the wrong flag, so she picked a pale green scarf instead.

She checked the roll of jewellery, the pieces Shahd had helped her choose, modelling every necklace, bracelet and ring. Shahd liked the more abstract ones, unlike Maisoon, who was more drawn to those inspired from stolen glances at old tiles, a flutter of Um Muhammad's hand stitched scarf, the design of an ancient carpet in her father's library. She paused at the lack of history mocking her from the black roll. Looking at her watch, she knew she was risking being late. She quickly replaced the abstract jewellery with pieces which held a secret story. There wasn't a particular category these pieces could be defined by. But she was content that she wasn't betraying herself, whatever the consequences.

On the bus, she sits towards the back next to a woman in her early fifties, with a bulging bag-on-wheels. Maisoon imagines her a professor of Russian literature in her native land, coming here with false dreams, ending up cleaning people's homes so that her children can attend university. Two soldiers, kids really, stand by the back doors; their weapons casually slung over their shoulders. Three teenagers in the back are listening to George Wassouf's 'Kalam Ennas' on an iPod. A blonde woman in her forties sits in front of the teenagers with a sour expression on her face.

The clear, bell-like voice of Fairouz replaces the scratchy one of

19

George Wassouf, singing 'Habbaytak fi Essayf'. The boys are quarrelling about a game of basketball, their voices rising, bouncing back from the roof, the blonde woman's expression now tightly-packed disgust. The Russian woman shifts in her seat, mumbling something to the window. Maisoon sings softly along with Fairouz, her eyes transfixed on the slow, unconscious movements of the right hand of one of the soldiers as he caresses his machine gun, stroking its dull, metallic curves. These movements are repeated by the second soldier. Together, the two hands are performing a sacred dance, bowing to the power embodied in those pieces slung so indifferently across their shoulders.

The blonde woman turns sharply around and in a shrill voice demands that the boys turn the music off. The boys snicker and turn the music down a notch.

But that doesn't satisfy her, "Don't you understand Hebrew? This is public transport and I shouldn't have to listen to this on my way to work!"

Maisoon shifts in her chair to speak up, but someone else beats her to it. Surprised, she hears the strong voice of the Russian woman, struggling with her heavily accented Hebrew, red cherries rising to her face.

"Why can't you just let them be? They're not disturbing anybody. Can't you enjoy the beautiful music? I'm sure if it were Jewish boys listening to music in Hebrew you'd be sitting there quietly. It's because they're Arab, right?"

The red cherries now jump to the cheeks of the blonde woman, "Who asked for your opinion? And who asked you to come here in the first place? Go back to your Russia."

Maisoon watches the Russian woman weigh her options before opting for a thin smile. The boys are now sitting in silence, looking straight ahead as if the conversation didn't concern them. The music is turned down another notch, but still playing. Maisoon is glad they haven't turned it off. The blonde woman is sitting with tightly drawn lips, upset that nobody came to her rescue. When the Russian woman

20

makes to get up, Maisoon touches her hand and whispers thanks, "Toda."

A smile flutters over the woman's face and she shrugs her shoulders.

A few stops later, Maisoon stands and makes her way to the back door. People are pressed around her. She keeps her eyes on the weapons, making sure there is some distance between herself and them.

Ten minutes later she walks down a sleepy side street of Carmel Center and stops outside the number on the card. She takes a deep breath before entering the spacious boutique. The high ceilings, spotless walls and glass shelving tell Maisoon she won't find anything cheap within. Amalia, her silver hair elegantly framing her thin face, is busy with two women showing them a variety of necklaces with gemstones.

"Shalom, Giveret Amalia," Maisoon tries not to disturb them; from the bits of conversations reaching her she could tell these were regular customers.

"Shalom. I'll be with you in a moment. You can start arranging your pieces on that table over there."

Maisoon begins placing the jewellery on the table. Suddenly, they all look wrong. *I shouldn't have changed them. Should have trusted Shahd's choice.* Looking around her, she sees exquisite pieces. *She'll never take any of mine.* She is tempted to shove everything back into her backpack and disappear. She takes a deep breath and begins to group the jewellery, earrings, followed by bracelets, necklaces and finally rings. Unsatisfied, she rearranges them again. The two women are now leaving, without having bought anything.

"They can't make up their mind. It's a wedding present." Amalia now stands on the other side of the table, studying the jewellery, "Are you finished?" she smiles at no one in particular.

"Yes," Maisoon is watching Amalia but she has no idea whether she likes the pieces or not.

After a long silence, the older woman lets out a thin slice of air through her nostrils, "I think I need some time to look at them more

21

closely. They're not what I expected."

Maisoon holds her breath.

"I can't make up my mind. Why don't you give me, say, an hour?"

At a nearby café, Maisoon called Ziyad, who didn't seem to understand that it was possible for her to lose this opportunity. He tried to soothe her by telling her that she was a great designer and that the old lady was just trying to intimidate her.

"I have to go. Talk to you later." He was useless in calming her down, just like the lukewarm cappuccino she was sipping.

Back at the boutique, Amalia was on the phone, "Yes, darling, you'll have that cheese cake waiting for you on Shabbat. Now I have to go. Kisses." As she replaced the receiver with an elegant move Maisoon noticed the translucent moonstone on her ring finger.

"I just wanted to know how it feels," Amalia said. She took it off and put it back near the set of moonstone earrings.

They stood side by side looking down at the jewellery, Maisoon waiting.

"They're very unusual," the older woman finally said, "I'd go as far as saying eccentric. I don't like taking chances—I only go for solid, certain sale."

"I understand, Giveret Amalia."

"Really, now. Would you stop calling me Giveret? Please, just Amalia."

Maisoon bent down to open her backpack.

"Wait, Misun." It was the first time she had said Maisoon's name; with no clients around the name was unthreatening.

"It's Maisoon," her hand stopped halfway into her backpack.

"I'll make a deal with you. You choose eight pieces—two of each. You can have that small shelf in the corner. That plant needs some fresh air anyway and I've been meaning to take it home for a while. You can arrange them by yourself." Her voice was business-like, a tinge of pity in it. "If I sell anything, you get 70 percent. Oh, and you decide on the price. The lowest prices here are 350 shekels."

22

If she weren't so formal, Maisoon would have hugged her. She settled for a weak smile and a "thank you very much, Amalia," and quickly began arranging the jewellery.

When she was finished, Amalia stood behind her, a smile brushing her lips.

"And the prices?"

"Oh, I really don't know, 380 for each?"

"I hope you're not that cheap with men," Amalia didn't try to conceal her smile now. "Call me in two weeks to see if I've sold anything."

Maisoon was halfway out the door when Amalia added "Oh, and one more thing. You have one month. If nothing sells by then, we're done doing business."

حيفا فراجمنتس

The smell of Ziyad's famously delicious shakshooka reached her nostrils as she took the steps in twos, realizing she was famished. For once, she was glad he'd invaded her apartment.

They ate lunch in silence, Ziyad wanting to avoid anything that had to do with checkpoints and little sick kids, while Maisoon was annoyed that he didn't ask how her meeting had gone. Things were getting complicated between them. Something Maisoon had made every effort to avoid. She just wanted a lover. Nothing more. Not now. But Ziyad wanted a wife. Nothing less. To break the silence, Maisoon brought a bottle of cheap red wine from the kitchen.

"Mashallah! You made a deal with the Yahudiyya?" Ziyad's face lit up.

"She let me have a shelf," she said, not looking at his face, "You know, for display."

Ziyad's hand froze mid-air between the bottle and his glass. He thought of the long hours she spent glued to her worktable. "Walla? Mabrouk ya hayati!" He tried to sound excited, but Maisoon knew that inside, his sense of worthlessness was expanding.

Ziyad had finished his degree in architecture at the Technion two years ago but hadn't found a proper job. Most Jewish companies didn't want an Arab employee and in the Arab community, things were complicated. Strings had to be pulled, you had to have the right connections, the right family name and, sometimes even the right religion. For two years now, he'd been working at the customer service department of a cellular phone company, occasionally giving private lessons in maths and physics to high school students.

"It's just a small shelf, barely visible. And she's giving me a month. But I know she didn't really like my work." Maisoon tried to soften the blow. "But hey! You want to see what I'm working on now?" Grabbing her glass of wine, she got up and started in the direction of the large wooden worktable.

Ziyad came up behind her, grabbing her around the waist, taking away her glass, whispering in her ear, "Later, hayati. We should first do something wild."

Maisoon heard a tinge of sadness in his voice.

After making love, they fell asleep, exhausted. When they woke up, it was already dark outside. Another day almost gone. Um Tawfiq would be checking on her laundry. Abu Nidal would be making the last pot of kahwa for the day and Um Muhammad would be on her way home. And Maisoon and Ziyad would be ...

حيفا فراجمنتس

Later that evening, when the suffocating heat subsided, they took a cool shower and left for a café. The souk was now only a ghost of faint scents—vegetables mingled with the bitterness of kahwa, wrapping loosely around Maisoon's scarf. It was yet to produce the thick rotting smells that would rise later. They walked in silence. Not hand in hand. Not in Wadi Nisnas. Maisoon in one of her long summer skirts, a red scarf draped over her white tanktop. The crumbling two-storey buildings on each side of the narrow alley were leaning close to one another, the greying white cracks between the stones widening up just so, whispering almost-forgotten, bruised memories.

"So what's the deal with this Yahudiyya? Why did you say before that she didn't like your work?" Ziyad asked as they walked up the stairs marking the end of the souk.

"I don't know. It's just that … I felt she let me have that undusted shelf out of pity. And my work looked so out of sync with the rest of the jewellery. I mean, you should see what she's got in there!" She adjusted her scarf, blown off her shoulders by a light naseem. "The jewellery she sells is so boring, it's all the same, with clean sharp lines."

"Think positive, Mais. That's probably why she liked your work. Because it's fresh and different."

It was his logical mode of thinking, so simple yet so distanced from her. It's what attracted her to him but also what frustrated her. He was very practical and rational. Not emotional like her. He had solid feet on the ground. An anchor. Blueprints ready for a whole lifetime.

At the café, they were interrupted by a phone call from Tamar. Maisoon excused herself and walked outside. These phone calls were all too familiar to Ziyad. Maisoon would sometimes be on the phone for more than an hour with her Jewish friends. 'Sharing' as Maisoon put it. After the phone call, and for the rest of their evening, Maisoon talked about Machsom Watch while Ziyad sipped his beer in silence, his calm face belying his annoyance. Can't I have even one single night with you. You alone. Just give me one night without checkpoints, soldiers, permits, crossing borders, the chasm between this world and theirs. Is that too much to ask of you, Mais?

"I'll walk you home, but I'm not coming up."

She turned around, noticing only now that he was walking a few steps behind her. She looked away—knowing a lie was forming on his lips.

"I promised Basel to help him with this project he needs to submit at the end of the month. I have to be at his place early in the morning."

Maisoon kept walking, increasing the distance between them.

25

"But I can be at your place for lunch tomorrow … I'll make you a nice shakshooka." He caught up with her, touched the small of her back, but her body evaded him. The rest of the way to the souk passed in silence.

He kissed her lightly and turned around, without salamat. She grabbed him by his shirt and pulled him to her. Their bodies collided, the cold stone against her back. Warmth spreading down her legs. His tongue on her neck. Fingers invading her belly, stealing their way downwards. Feeling the muscles of his back tense at the touch of her palms. The very subtle groan—almost a whisper—released involuntarily with his outbreath.

Two teenage boys were approaching, their laughter pushing the wind ahead of them. She cupped his face in her palms, kissed him violently, pushed his body away, and disappeared into the dark stairway. "No shakshooka tomorrow. I want a restaurant. Good night albi." Her voice tumbled down from the top of the stairs with the same force as her kiss.

# 4

Amalia called three weeks later. "Maisun? Shalom, it's Amalia. You didn't call, I hope everything is all right with you? Anyway, next week will be one month, but I think you should come and speak with me before." Her voice was again that clean sheet of newly polished gemstone, impossible to read. "So, can you come at one o'clock?"

It was eleven thirty and Maisoon still hadn't dressed, her hair was a mess and Ziyad's smell was all over her. Not one piece sold. She wants me to clear up the shelf.

"Shai?" Ziyad's voice brought her back up from the depths she was sinking into.

"Come with me, Ziyad. Maybe we can go down to the beach after," she said into her cup of shai.

"I think I'll just stay here and wait for you." He saw the worry in her eyes. "Hey! Don't jump to any conclusions. Maybe she sold everything and she wants to commission more? If she does, then we'll go out and celebrate tonight. Ach, a bottle of wine, just you and me, the rocks and the sea. Yalla, khalas, smile habibti. It will be all right, Inshallah."

Inshallah. Inshallah. How she envied him his faith at such times. Inshallah. If God wills.

The trip to Amalia's Jewellery seemed to take forever. I will try some boutiques in Nazareth or Akka next week. Still immersed in her plans when she walked in, her thoughts were caught by the absence of a single ring; it was the one Amalia had tried on three weeks ago. So the lady pities me and bought it for herself. Or—maybe she likes it after all.

"Shalom, Amalia."

"Maisoon."

She got the name right this time. But she wasn't wearing the moonstone ring.

"Come, let's have a cup of coffee. My housecleaner brings me good Arabic coffee from her village, the best, really."

Amalia was smiling at Maisoon as they sipped their coffee. "Somebody bought that ring yesterday. A wedding present."

Maisoon remembered the two women from last time.

"A young man was interested in one of the necklaces for his wife—an anniversary present—but he said it looked too ... how did he put it, traditional, too heavy, for his wife's taste."

Maisoon just nodded, uncertain where this was leading.

"I think I will give you a chance. Like I said, the pieces are too unusual for my taste, but we'll try for another month. You can have that big window over there. Two shelves."

Maisoon looked disbelievingly in the direction of the window; it was still in the farthest corner. A narrow one, but it was a window. All to herself.

"This is yours. 70 percent." She handed Maisoon an envelope.

"But this is 500 shekels, Amalia ..."

"Well, you can't expect me to sell this kind of jewellery for the ridiculous price of 380!" her smile broadened.

Maisoon leaned forward to hug Amalia but stopped herself. Instead, she reached out and closed her hand on Amalia's fragile fingers. "Thank you so much, Amalia. You're wonderful!"

She felt Amalia's hand jerk back for a fraction of a second before

28

loosening up. That pulling back was almost enough to
doubts, to keep a wall between their worlds.

But Amalia said softly, "Even though it's not my p...
have to admit you're an amazingly talented artist." It was the
anyone had used the word artist in relation to Maisoon.

Waiting for the underground Carmelit to reach the Carmel mountain,
she called Ziyad. "One bottle of wine, one big rock, a piece of the sea
and the sky of night please."

"On my eye and on my head, ya hayati."

Over the next month, almost half of Maisoon's jewellery sold. After two
months, she was given one of the three large showcases inside the
boutique. It was also then that Amalia asked her if she could come twice
a week to replace her in the afternoons, "for a modest salary," was how
she put it.

Ziyad would dangle this news in front of his friends like a trophy
he'd won. Except it wasn't a trophy. And it wasn't his. Maisoon felt that
under those boisterous grand words lay a wounded pride about his own
impotence. He was still working shifts, earphones on, calming down
furious clients, giving away free air-time in response to their threats to
move to the competitor's cell-phone company.

بيتنا فراجمنتسي

Layla is ecstatic about her daughter's small steps in the real world. Majid
stays quiet, he is still upset at Maisoon for abandoning medical school
but he has no power over this or her choice of a partner. Maisoon asks
them to drop by the boutique, hoping that he will see that she hasn't
thrown away her future. But her father doesn't join her mother as she
enters the shop. Instead he waits in the car while Layla unleashes her
exultation in unreserved mashallahs and ya salams, much to the alarm
of the one client who quickly disappears.

29

Majid looks through the car window as Layla links arms with their daughter and is led around the shop. Maisoon working for this Yahudiyya ... she could have done much better. He fumbles in the console for his cigarettes and lighter. His lungs pull the smoke deep inside, he holds it before forcing it out. As it hits the glass he thinks about his own career, if he can call it that.

He ended up a clerk in a bank, working overtime most days, correcting the mistakes of others, mentoring all the new clerks. In the first few years, he trusted his abilities, strongly believing that he would get promoted—every year he'd tell the family "Next year for sure." But—next year never came. He watched as those same clerks he welcomed and taught climbed up the ladder, becoming heads of departments, one even becoming his own boss. Oh, but he did get compliments. All the time. How professional he was, how responsible; a pat on the back every now and then, a bonus twice a year. But nothing more. Because he didn't belong. Because his name was Majid.

And he accepted it, for he was of the generation today called the subservient. Those who never dared raise their heads. Those who grew up under military rule; fear becoming an inseparable part of their very essence.

Maisoon had never known her father in any other way. To her, he had always been the meek, obedient citizen, making an effort to be as inconspicuous as he could be with his choice of clothes, behaviour, the radio stations he listened to in the car. Or the way he lowered his voice when pronouncing his name. Very rarely, when he felt extra brave, he'd put on Fairouz but he would turn it off when they neared a public space with security guards.

# 5

Maisoon's mother opened the door to a strong smell of Arabic kahwa, "Mais habibti! What a surprise!" Layla was a plump woman in her late fifties with long black hair splashed with silver. She was almost always smiling and her eyes sparkled when she greeted people. On that morning she was wearing a deep purple housedress with black and red hand-stitched designs. Majid had bought if for her when they went to Jenin years ago to visit friends. That was a lifetime ago. Though Layla still mentioned to her husband every now and again that she'd love to go back, Majid wouldn't hear of it. It's not safe these days. End of discussion. And Layla would fall silent, until next time.

Mother and daughter embraced in the doorway. When Layla had inhaled enough of her daughter's fresh smell, she led her by the hand towards the kitchen, "I just made myself some good kahwa; strong just the way you like it. Lots of sugar too."

"So, habibti, there must be something that brought you here, you wouldn't come and visit just like that, with you so busy lately," Layla poured kahwa into Maisoon's favourite cup, the cracked one she refused to take with her but didn't allow her mother to throw away.

"I'm stuck with this design I've been working on, and needed to get away from it, so I thought I'd drop by and pick up some of my stuff."

Layla lifted her cup and inhaled. "Now for the kahwa to come out just right, you have to boil it seven times. Each time it starts rising furiously, you take it off the flames, let it calm down, and then again bring it to a raging boil … seven times, not six, not eight …"

Maisoon giggled as she listened to the words her mother had told her countless times when she was a child.

"And still my kahwa is the best in Haifa," Layla added with a mischievous smile.

They sat at the kitchen table for a while, Maisoon told Layla about bits of her life, avoiding anything that involved Ziyad, military checkpoints and special permits. "And Baba is still angry with Tayseer? Hasn't forgiven him yet?"

Sadness snuck into Layla's eyes, "He will habibti. He'll forgive him … Right after he forgives himself." Her face was locked into that same blank expression she wore lately whenever they discussed Majid. Maisoon sensed that her parents were growing apart and that she was partly to blame.

"Now Mais, you go ahead and get the stuff you need. I'm going out to visit Um Talal. You have the house key with you, right?" Layla didn't wait for an answer, she pushed herself up and headed to her bedroom to change.

Alone in the cool stone house, Maisoon took her kahwa outside to the garden and sat under the grapevine. In her mind, she heard her father's strong voice drilling into her and Tayseer, you'll be a doctor. And you, you will become a lawyer, you'll wear smart suits and I will buy you a leather suitcase. You'll make me proud. Tayseer would then walk through the garden, his five-year-old face screwed up into seriousness, a plastic briefcase at his side. Maisoon would listen to her father's breathing with a plastic stethoscope. For them, it was a game. For Majid, they were rehearsing their future roles. Roles they would never enact. Tayseer only had the courage to stand up to their father after Maisoon did. It was Maisoon who put down the stepping stones and for that, Baba would never forgive her.

She carried her cup inside and rinsed it in the sink. As she walked past the family library she remembered she wanted to grab a book to read. She scanned the new arrivals, resting her eyes on Mahmoud Darwish's *Jidariyya*. She scribbled a note to let her father know she'd borrowed it, signing the first letter of her name, the meem— م—like she used to when she was a child—her favourite letter when it was at the end of a word, because it looked like a small flower. She then headed into her old bedroom, and took down several boxes from the closet. Settling comfortably on the threadbare carpet, she started sifting through the materials, one box at a time. Drawings from kindergarten (keep for Mother), exams from high school (throw away), notes passed during class (decide later), birthday cards (throw away). Seminar papers from her first (and only) year at medical school (definitely burn), old school photographs (leave here for now), big, bulging brown envelopes (put in the stack to decide later), postcards from friends in different parts of the world (keep), newspaper clippings (leave here to go through when there is more time). More bulging brown envelopes she didn't recognize.

Maybe her mother went over some of her things and began organizing them, putting things in envelopes. She emptied the contents of the first envelope onto the carpet. Old photographs she had never seen before curled at the edges in despair. Letters, postcards and pieces of paper in different sizes. Is this the history of Majid and Layla's love? She smiled at the thought. She looked through the photographs, expecting to see her mother and father both posing for the camera. There was definitely her father in the photos. Young, lean, with those piercing eyes and a determination made of rock. A woman's delicate hand was wrapping his kafiyyah around his shoulders. She studied his young face, her own crooked smile grinning back at her. She could sense that this man was and was not her father. His spirit unbroken, promises of great things to come. Above all, full of playful determination. It was in the way he cocked his head towards the camera.

She turned to the yellowing pages. She could tell by the handwriting that most of them were written in haste, as if the writer were trying to catch that last train to Damascus. She recognized Majid's handwriting; being left-handed, it had a noble curl to it. Forbidden love letters written to the ravishing Layla? Maisoon felt her heart quicken as she began reading. No love history here either. They were notes about the taste of the brown earth, the scattered stones of a destroyed home, mud on a man's boots. There was something off in the words, something not quite falling into sync. She started reading again, from the beginning, but this time aloud. And there it was—music. The words were lilting on her tongue like the soft notes of oud. Like the movement of the petals of a flower in a gentle naseem. Poetry tucked into the form of prose. Baba, the bank clerk? A poet? Could it be? The same father who almost disowned his son when he quit law school to enrol in music studies? The same father who was angry about her political activities—himself writing about resistance? She turned the idea from one side of her mind to the other, but it refused to settle like sand grains after a desert storm. She put the photos and the writings back into the envelopes and straight into her bag.

حيفا فراجمنتس

Now, two weeks later, the envelopes sit unopened in her desk drawer—she has been reluctant to stir up her father's past. Leafing absent-mindedly through the book on Palestinian traditional dress, one of the photos catches her eye—there is something familiar about the dress. It reminds her of another dress. Where has she seen it before? In another photograph of a different era. A young woman with long black hair spread like the wings of a bird on her chest. And then it comes to her. Yes, of course it's one of the photographs of her father with a young woman. They hold hands and look straight into the camera.

Enough work for today. She closes the book and puts it on top of her sketchbook. Taking the envelopes out of the desk drawer, she spreads their contents on the floor. First, she separates the papers from

34

the photographs. She is intrigued by the prose poetry so she decides to start with that.

The first poem is about land and sumud. Rootedness. Images of the ancient olive tree in an ancient land. Refusal to leave. Resistance. The next few pages she picks up are notes scribbled on napkins—more sumud. There are also allusions to violent resistance. She feels like an intruder. The writer of these words is a complete stranger to her. She struggles to reconcile the fierce, defiant person behind the words with the resigned man of today.

A piece of paper with a single word—أسمهان. Asmahan. Written in beautiful Arabic calligraphy. The letters are curling in various directions, making intricate patterns. The design is as much part of the word as the letters themselves. She searches through the rest of the papers, quickly scanning for more references to Asmahan. Now she has at least two central themes, she separates the poems, prose and letters into two heaps. One heap—sumud and resistance. The other—Asmahan.

She picks up an Asmahan piece when she is jerked back into the present by the phone.

"Where are you? I've been sitting here for half an hour, waiting for you! Or did you forget me again?" Ziyad's voice rises in a furious wave over the clamour of the café.

What day is it anyway? She hasn't seen him for at least a week, and he is beginning to dissipate somewhere into the background of her life. "No, no, I didn't forget you, habibi. It's just that ... I'll be right there." There is no point in trying to explain it to him. What would she tell him anyway? Oh, just discovered my father was a poet. Yes, the same father who almost disowned Tayseer ... and me.

ديفا فراجمنتس

Maisoon returns home a couple of hours later, drops her bag on the floor and sinks onto the diwan. He wants to own part of her world. He wants to put a mahbas on her finger. محبس m a h b a s. She turns the letters on her tongue, stressing the *ha'a*. From the root habasa. Imprisoned. He wants to confine her—no less than with a shackle of gold around her finger. So that the whole world knows she belongs to a man. Not to herself. Yes, she's ready to give up some inconsequential liberties. But not her right to freedom.

To dance at four in the morning. To wash the dishes once every other day. Only. To have her morning kahwa with a cigarette on her narrow balkon under the clothes hanging to dry. In her father's gallabiyya. To clean the house only once every two weeks. To make love at noon. Sometimes right before dinner. (And why not?) To eat fresh fruit for lunch. To read a book all night long while the birds are tucked away in the darkness. To draw in the morning. To take pictures of the souk in mid-afternoon, bursting with colour.

No. She won't be able to do these things if she is to wear a mahbas. Not in her way. And Ziyad will not understand. His concept of freedom clashes with hers.

Maisoon rubs the back of her neck; she needs to think about something else for a while. She gets off the diwan and fetches her father's papers. Picking up a random piece, she studies the words. The letters are gliding across, the *seen*, losing its three teeth and just flattened, the two dots under the *ya* becoming a thin line, in the haste of putting down the words that follow.

After that, it was a long time before you started coming back—piece by piece. First, it was the scent of your hair that slowly, elusively, entered into my dreams. Then, the inscription of your breath on my eyelids. Each dream brought another piece of you back, until finally your name appeared. In beautiful calligraphy of course. And that's when I knew you were real. They erased you from my mind—yes, utterly and completely. But love is lodged somewhere else. And they could never erase you from my body.

36

She sat up straight in her chair and reread the last few lines. She couldn't decipher the meaning of it. Who did this to you, Baba?

She picked another one, with a title drawn in pencil. سامحني *Forgive me*. There was no indication of a date. The handwriting was steady, with all the dots neatly placed exactly in their designated places—above the *ta*, under the *ya*, in the hollow of the *noon*. There were no shortcuts here with the *seen* and *sheen* either—they all had their three teeth neatly drawn just at the right angle.

*Forgive me.*                                              سامحني

So today they finally got you.
Last time we smoked nargila together you laughed. You said, they'll never get you.
But they did.
You said, "Who's interested in a fighter whose weapon is the pencil?"
But they were.
You said, they can't get you yet. Not before you write the greatest story for Palestine.
But they didn't wait.

I ask your forgiveness today, my brother. You said, "We'll put our two weapons together and fight hand in hand—you like the chewing potential of the pencil, while I opted for the permanence of ink." But you've gone now and I have nothing left. So. I am putting my pen down. I'm tired, brother. I can't fight this fight any more.

First, they took away Asmahan.
Now you are gone too.
How much grief can one soul contain?
I am not in it to test my strength.

I will put my pen down after this. Never to pick it up again—not for this fight.

I want to gather what's left of me—these fragments of my life. No more fighting for a land that's lost.

Please forgive me, my brother. And see you somewhere on the other side of this madness, where we can finally write in peace. Salam from Haifa to wherever you may be.

Her tanktop stuck to her like glue. She peeled it off and lay back. Pushed the envelopes off the diwan onto the stone floor. Closed her eyes. It's as if I were physically digging through to get to you, Baba.

She dreams of walking into glass and passing through to the other side. She takes a few steps. Pauses. Listens to the strange silence. She turns around and the glass turns into see-through blocks. Dark hands—hundreds of them—are putting one block on top of the other. On the other side of the wall—Ziyad is standing, looking at her but not seeing. He is smiling. She smiles back at him and waves for him to cross over. When he doesn't react, she realizes he isn't smiling at her, but through her. She quickly turns around, but there's no one else. She's all alone on one side of the glass wall. She rushes at the wall and wakes up as her body shatters into shards of glass.

Maisoon sat up. Her breasts were crisscrossed with the pattern of the diwan's upholstery. She slid her legs over the side—something crinkled under her feet. Baba. She knelt down and gathered the scattered envelopes and loose pieces, piled them all in one corner of the diwan, and walked to the kitchen.

She came back to the salu, the rich aroma of strong kahwa trailing behind her. Settling herself and sipping slowly. She picked up some pages torn from a writing pad with the daunting heading *Israel Prison Service* at the top. A line crossed the bottom of each page with an address and a telephone number, a cold reminder of the real place. These were the only dated pages of all the writing. 1968. One year after the Six-Day War. That was when the Egyptians broadcast warnings in Hebrew over the radio. It was when the Jews prepared the Teddy stadium for mass

38

graves. In six days, Israel gained new territory. Countless Palestinians joined the already overflowing refugee camps. More tents were set up under the burning sun.

Been here for two weeks—or maybe two months? The Syrian fallaheen made us turn back. We almost made it home except we were all covered in mud and the taxi driver we thought was Arab turned out to be a Mizrahi Jew. Drove us straight to the military camp. Don't know if Amjad and Saif are somewhere in here too, or if they were let go. The only sunlight I have seen is from a crack in the corner, splitting the wall all the way through. Through here an echo of sunlight makes its way sadly into my room, casting a mourning reminder of life. Father and mother must be out of their minds. Don't even know if they were informed and aren't allowed to visit me. Maybe they were saved the grief of knowing. Can't feel my legs—can't remember what they did. It seems I was made to look straight into a burning light for an eternity. And after that, even when I closed my eyes, I still saw white light dancing behind my eyelids. And then they ... but I can't bring myself to write about that. No. How many days have passed since? What did I say? I am delirious. Demented. My body stretched beyond the limits of pain. I can't even remember her name. Did we ever kiss? Did I ever feel her breath on my cheek? Or did I make her up? I guess it's true all the stories about these places.

Not able to take in another word, she slammed the letter down. What horrors did they make him live through if his mind refused to remember even Asmahan? And how come her father hid his time in prison from her and Tayseer? She dialled Ziyad's number. "Can you meet me in Bat Galim in about an hour? No, I don't need a ride, I'll walk. I just ... I need ... some air."

حيفا فراجمنتس

39

The sea was purple, with a great orange ball drowning in it. Seeing Ziyad sitting on their rock with his back turned to her, she hurried, feeling a crumb of relief brushing the insides of her palms like so many grains of sand. He instantly knew by the movement of her body that she came to him in weakness, and opened his arms for her to enter into a silent hug. Her body felt drained, at once hollow and stiff.

"Let's take a walk," he whispered into her neck.

They walked in silence for a while, Maisoon's eyes on the horizon. And then it all spilled out. From the day she found the boxes in her old room.

It came out in tangles. Then slower. With more logic. Ziyad listened to her without asking any questions. He sensed her fear. History was being rewritten for her. When he felt she'd let loose all the words crammed into her body, he reached out to her and held her tight.

"Mais, this is just unreal."

She nodded her head, her cheek rubbing against his t-shirt.

"You know what? I think you shouldn't be afraid to find out. After all, you'll discover the real Majid. And from what you've told me so far, it seems to me your father is a great rajul. And you're only at the very beginning. And Asmahan? Well, don't tell me I'm your first love. What—you think Layla was the only woman in your father's life? Remember, he married her when he was almost forty, right? There were probably many more Asmahans before Layla."

For a moment, she was taken aback, shocked by her own naivety, trying to imagine her ageing father as a young man in love with this Asmahan. Then her mind zoomed back, to her life before Ziyad. Yes, she too had loved before.

They walked along the sand, the waves slapping the beach sounded like watermelons being split. They were lost in their own thoughts, their shadows merging and separating.

Almost home, Maisoon stopped. Turned around and started walking back. Now what? Ziyad followed in silence.

"Take me to that nargila place you go to sometimes, the one your friend Jihad has."

"Bas Maisoon! It's just a small place full of white smoke and sweaty men. No women."

Great! Just mumtaz.

"It's … it's sort of a closed club … and all they do is smoke, play shesh besh, talk politics and make up nonsense conspiracies." His words were carried backward up the mountain.

Maisoon continued to walk. I want to feel it. I want to sit and smoke a nargila like Majid did.

"And the chairs are really really uncomfortable!"

No response other than Maisoon's scarf swooshing behind her.

It was nothing like she expected. It wasn't even a nargila place. Jihad lived in a dilapidated stone house with the original dark green wooden shutters coming off their hinges. Ziyad opened the narrow heavy door and walked in without knocking. Maisoon had to force herself to follow his shadow; the high ceiling lent the long, narrow entrance an illusory sense of spaciousness.

"Yalla, ta'ali! What are you waiting for? A special uzumi?" Ziyad was opening a door at the other end of this outer room; yellow-grey light escaping from beyond and landing on the cream tiles. Dense smoke swirling around in the light.

She followed slowly, her courage discarded at the front door like shoes left at the entrance to a mosque. A cough, shaddi being thrown, shesh besh tiles moving around hectically, slapping down on the board. A sudden scratching of a chair and the movement of bodies as Ziyad walked in.

"Ahlaaaaaan ya Abu El-Hasan! Shu hal honour! We thought …" Maisoon's entrance caught the rest of the words in the man's throat. The body turned into stone, the mouth remained half-way open. Four heads raised, scanning the space between Ziyad and Maisoon. Drawing a line with their eyes.

"Assalamu Alaikum, shabab."

Ziyad didn't lose his balance, he laughed. "Ya salam, one sabiyya and you're off your tiles? And you call yourselves zlam!"

41

"You know this is no place for any sabaya, Abu El-Hasan," Jihad threw his shaddi and played his black tiles, closing off Mu'atasem's white. He looked at Maisoon sideways, his nod half an apology, half an acknowledgement of her boldness to enter this space reserved for men. Maisoon accepted his apology with a crooked smile of her own.

When the men realized the invader was there to stay, they settled back into their shesh besh game, grumbling under their breath. Maisoon found a frayed old smelly couch in one corner and settled down. Ziyad sat down in a wooden chair and watched the game, waiting for his turn to play. Soon Maisoon was forgotten and Mu'atasem continued with his interrupted stories of his prison days. In the darkness, he looked almost as old as Majid, and for several minutes Maisoon thought that she would get something, a thread. But when he mentioned some dates, she realized he couldn't be talking about the same period. She closed her eyes, absorbing the story which, all of a sudden turned into a tale of women and sexual journeys. She opened her eyes and looked at Ziyad—he was immersed in the game. She closed her eyes again, lowered her back on the couch, and dozed off. Dreamed of prisons and nymphs and deserts. The persistent ringing of her phone jerked her back into the room.

From the corner of his eye, Ziyad saw Maisoon stepping outside to the back garden, the phone to her ear, an unsettled look on her face. He watched her intently through the window, but the darkness obscured the expressions on her face. All he could see was her skirt pacing up and down, followed by the bluish smoke of a cigarette. And then another. Fifteen minutes and three cigarettes later, she walked back in. Sat on Ziyad's knees. Drank from his beer.

"Oh, I hate beer," she said, making a sour face.

"What was that all about?" He drew back as much as he could from her warm body.

"Shu? The phone call?" she now moved to a free chair next to him, seeing how awkward he felt with her sitting on his knees. In front of other men. "Oh, hayati, it was Shahd. She was telling me about this

42

cousin of hers from Khirbit Jbara. Some soldiers broke into his house last night." Her voice was brimming with anger. "Just like that, for no reason. They broke some furniture. Searched the house. Didn't give a reason. And they took all his research. He's been working on it for months. His pregnant wife was terrified ... she's bleeding and he doesn't know what to do." Her face was clouded, "Let's just go home, Ziyad. Min fadlak. I'm exhausted."

He had hoped she'd invite him up to her place—but she didn't. He had long since learned the single most important rule in their relationship—set in a silent pact. To always wait for her to invite him up. Never to impose himself on her private space. Though she didn't mind him having a key to her apartment and coming in when she wasn't home. But that was just another part of the subtle incongruity of their relationship. He stopped at the entrance to her building and waited.

"Not tonight. I need to be alone and think." She brushed his cheek with her lips and walked inside, leaving behind the echo of two words, "maybe tomorrow."

# 6

ﻉ Even their first meeting had been out of kilter. It was a Friday night, and Ziyad and his friends were smoking nargila on the Camel beach in Haifa. It was around nine in the evening, and the promenade was barely containing all the young couples, families, groups of teenagers, and older couples. A fusion of tanktops, bikinis, headscarves, jeans, elegant dresses, training suits. High heels, flip-flops, sneakers, sandals and bare feet. Arabic and Hebrew and Russian, with the occasional English or German rising up. An atmosphere of sexual tension. Of wet sand in your shoes and between your toes and under your tongue. Shesh besh on the beach. Nargila on the grass. All summer long. The perfect place to meet young women. But that summer, Ziyad wasn't looking for a woman. All his energy was invested in finding a job, he had just gotten his degree in architecture.

"Look at these three! They're Muslim. Aseel, ask them where they're from." Haitham was the youngest of the three, and the first one to get excited over any walking headscarf.

"Just leave it, min shan Allah," Ziyad said with growing impatience, taking the nargila from Aseel's hand with an annoyed expression.

"What's the matter with you? No harm done in some fun," Aseel stared at the young women as they passed by, screwing up his best smile. "And anyway, we'll behave in a perfectly dignified way! You think I'll risk staining their honour?" He looked insulted.

Ziyad kept silent, slowly blowing the smoke into the salty, humid air. It wasn't worth getting into arguments about 'honour' with his friends. They all knew what he thought of the ancient belief that a family's honour lay between a woman's legs. But every time he tried arguing, he was pushed back into silence. There was no arguing with tradition. So he learned to swallow it along with the smoke of the apple nargila.

His mind floated as he stared out towards the black sea with its slow-forming white foaming waves. People were walking on the shore, sandals slung over shoulders. Suddenly, he felt suffocated. The shallowness of it all—sitting there with his friends, smoking nargila, hunting for some one-night adventure of a sensual nature. Everybody did it. They all played along. They all knew the rules. They all were from 'good families'. Yet they all were here. Enjoying a bit of freedom without compromising their 'families' honour'. It was a dangerous game … but the suspended danger made it all the more thrilling. Except that Ziyad no longer wanted to be part of it. He wanted something else. Something solid.

"I'm going for a walk on the beach. Don't wait for me, I'll take a taxi home. Salamat." He walked to the end of the promenade, where the asphalt gave way to the sand and bent to take off his shoes.

The sand felt warm between his toes. He tried to remember the last time he'd been to the beach to swim, but couldn't. He walked slowly trying to get his balance right, his feet sinking with each step. He moved closer to the water. Soon he was hypnotised by the dark beauty of the sea, his mind emptied by the sound of the waves, at once sharp and soothing.

Slowly the sound of drumming mixed with the waves. He peered through the dark. Small specks, scattered in a circle—like stones made for a fire. As he approached, they grew larger. Men and women, some sitting on blankets, others on the sand. Some standing, swaying their bodies to the rhythm of the drums. The music stopped. Ziyad stayed there, awkwardly, a feeling of intrusion crumpling underneath his skin until he noticed that he was not the only one watching. Several people were gathered around, a bit distanced from the group.

The music started again. Arabic music. Something on the verge of the familiar. Ziyad heard the distinct, sharp sound of the durbakki. A woman. Dragged into the circle by another woman, who hurriedly tied a scarf around her waist. "Yalla, habibti, yalla ya amar, let your mind slip out of your head."

She slowly walked to the middle of the circle; Ziyad imagined her eyes closed. He couldn't tell, it was too dark. Her head was bent down, as if she were shy and just about to walk away. The drums faded into a rhythmic monotonous beat, the durbakki above them all in sharp, tantalizing notes. She began to sway ever so gently. The durbakki was teasing her. A few moments passed and her body began to move, taking on a life of its own. In complete harmony with the music and the waves, she was slowly becoming a shadow, losing her physical body. Ziyad was riveted, mesmerized by this dancing shadow. It wasn't belly dancing as he knew it. She was improvising, creating new moves, sliding along with the beat of the drums, with the sound of the waves.

She seemed so free, with her red skirt flailing in the soft damp naseem, the scarf on her hips shimmering, green and orange streaks, shaking with each movement, shedding all constraints. It seemed unreal to him that someone—a woman—could be so unafraid to shatter the protecting wall they had all built around their souls.

He knew it was impossible to find a woman like that in his village. This dream belonged to someone else. Not someone weighed down by ancient cultural codes. She didn't belong in his world. Nor could he ever belong in hers. This last thought startled him, slowly settling in a corner of his mind like the sand under his toenails—stubborn.

The music stopped. The shadow transformed once again into a woman. "Ya salam! Tayseer, can you give me ya habibi ya eini? Durbakki solo. Yalla."

Ziyad blinked. She was speaking Arabic ... She was Arab! Her voice was somewhat smoky, not the silky soft he'd imagined it to be. He watched her, captivated, trying to fit her into a rational slot in his brain.

46

She was now dancing as if in a trance. She seemed unaware of the sensuousness enveloping her every movement. Ziyad was in a daze.

He didn't even realize that he was waiting. For the dancing to end so he could approach her. To tell her what? That she was as mysterious as the sea? That he needed solid ground and not this quicksand? That he needed to make a completely new slot in his brain so that she could fit into it? She was a stranger. Yet something compelled him to remain there, to make an effort to move towards her.

When the music stopped, she walked to the man with the durbakki, Tayseer, her hips still swaying to an unheard melody, gave him a hug and whispered to him. He was smiling at her. She kissed him on the cheek. Then took off for the sea, losing her skirt and scarf on the way. Her laughter was wild. Ziyad thought she might be a bit drunk. In black underwear and a white tanktop, she walked knee-deep and then dropped, the waves pushing past her, rocking her gently. She stayed like that for a few minutes before returning to the beach.

She put on her skirt and went to help a boy pack up a small drum. Her movements were at once delicate and fast. She murmured something to the boy and they both laughed. Again, her laughter had a smoky tinge to it. With confidence he didn't realize he had, Ziyad walked up to her just as she was brushing away some sand from the boy's hair.

"Salam," his own voice sounded scratchy.

"Hey," she smiled at him. A thin, crooked smile.

"I, uh ..." he was lost.

"You enjoyed the music?"

"I ... I just ..." he looked back, for something. What? To hold on to, he was sinking. Into the sand. Into her large brown eyes. "How come you dance so ..." he couldn't find the words.

"It's the simplest thing once you learn how to let go of all you're carrying around with you." She looked him straight in the eyes.

He didn't know what to say. He wasn't carrying anything around with him. "What are you carrying around with you?"

47

"Me?" She was taken aback. The wind blew her shoulder-length hair into her face. Unconsciously, she lifted her hand and tucked a strand behind her ear. He noticed specks of sand on her left cheek. He could tell it was she who was now racking her brain for the right words. But he was wrong. The words came slowly, with a sad but definitive tune to them, "It's this insane reality," she said, fixing her eyes on the black sea.

His next words came out before he could think. "I have to see you again."

She looked back at the little boy now picking up beer cans and water bottles abandoned by their owners. When she turned back to him, her face was glazed with exhaustion. "If you give me a good reason, I promise I'll think about it." She was ruthless. Made him think too hard.

"I … I want to understand what you mean by insane reality." He held his breath.

She turned to move. He was losing her. She began walking slowly towards the boy, picking up a plastic bag on her way. Ziyad almost turned around to go back. But he didn't move. And then it came. That smoky voice again, only a few feet away from him. She was sitting on the wet sand, her feet touching the water. She was speaking to the sea.

"Wadi Nisnas. Thursday morning. Find Um Muhammad at the souk and ask for me."

He stood still, sinking deeper into the sand. He tasted salt in his mouth, sand between his teeth. She got up and started walking away from him. "And your name?"

"Maisoon," she said to the wind, not bothering to look back.

هيفا فراجمنتس

On his way back, he could no longer hear the waves. Maisoon. Just forget about her. She was this Tayseer's girl. But then why did she tell him about the souk? Was it some twisted joke? I'm not going there on Thursday. Or any other day. Except for shopping. If she meant it, she'd have mentioned a specific time and more details. There must be at least three or four Um Muhammads in the souk. Was this Um Muhammad a vegetable vendor? Did Maisoon work for her? Enough. Forget her.

On Thursday, Ziyad was up by dawn. He was going to the souk today. Shopping. Two cups of coffee and three changes of jeans later, he was on his way to Wadi Nisnas. I'll just get some apples, tomatoes and baladi cucumbers.

He came back to his apartment towards noon, with no apples, no tomatoes and no baladi cucumbers either.

His roommate threw him a curious look, "So, you've met her, I suppose?"

# 7

ي You should ask him. You have the right to know your father. One day it will be too late. She is repeating the words Ziyad drilled into her brain the night before as she walks the short distance from her apartment to her parents' house. From the kitchen she spots her father in the garden and immediately pictures herself as the fragile baba's girl who would grow up to become a doctor. She winces at the image and at the thought of letting him down. There were many more disappointments that followed. He couldn't—wouldn't—bring himself to see her as capable of creating a successful future in any other way.

He is sitting in his usual corner of the garden, smoking a cigarette under the shade of the grapevine. Maisoon can see the sheib in his hair—white curly hairs peeking effortlessly through the thick black maze. Every time she comes to visit there seem to be more of them. Ziyad is right, there is no forever. "Marhaba, yaba," she greets him with a smile and a detached kiss on his cheek.

"Ahlan, habibti, ahlan," he seems surprised to see her, a sudden spark in his eyes makes him look younger than his sixty-seven years.

She has the urge to justify herself for not visiting for the past several months, but restrains herself. It was, after all, his disapproval of her having a partner of a different religion that had kept her away. "Where's Mama? Is she resting?" She pours herself a finjan of kahwa. Always an extra finjan for unexpected visitors. There are things she can't help but love about tradition. These gestures that make her feel part of something warm, ancient. There is not a Palestinian home where there's not that extra finjan. Unlike most Arab men, Majid loves to cook kahwa, but he never counts the seven times. Sometimes it is less, other times more. His kahwa never tastes the same; he likes to experiment with different amounts of kahwa, cardamom, and sugar.

"How are you, Mais? Mama is visiting Um Suleiman. She told me you took the book on Palestinian traditional dress from our library." He hands her a cigarette.

"Yes … I'm experimenting … I want to design some pieces that have a past. Our past."

He gives her a sad smile. "Mais, why are you so enmeshed in the past? It's gone, our land is gone, and we are citizens of this state. You can't bring back the past. It's dead."

"Actually, I wanted to ask you about that. I was looking for some of my papers and I found … well, these envelopes … with letters … and photographs in them. Really old."

He is looking at her intently, pinning her into silence with his dark eyes. He is struggling to keep calm and Maisoon immediately regrets telling him.

"I don't want to talk about it. I don't know how you came across them, though I can imagine … and I don't know how much you've read but …" His hands are shaking, he sucks on his cigarette, it fails to calm him. "You have no right to them!"

Just then Layla walks through the darkened garden. One look at the sullen faces of her husband and daughter tells her all she needs to know. She calls Maisoon inside for a cup of hot shai with fresh na'ana.

Maisoon watches her mother move around the kitchen stopping to fuss over her and ask about her life. She is so taken aback by her father's response that she doesn't say anything about it to Layla. Not yet. She'll have to think about it first. As her mother refills her cup she wonders what secrets are hidden in the folds of her heart. All of a sudden, it

51

seems natural that Layla also carries a small pouch containing her past. Life didn't start for Layla and Majid when they met. She tries to look at her mother with a stranger's eyes. Yes, there must be another life—another Layla—somewhere in her too.

Walking back to her apartment in the dark, her father's words reverberate. You have no right to them. For some reason, her thoughts take her back to a kaleidoscope he'd given her as a child. She had developed an obsession with it, looking through it in different light settings, ultimately using it as the basis for some of her designs. But it never crossed her mind to tell her father that she still looked through it. She feels a dull pain at the change in their relationship. It wasn't only her father who distanced himself from her; she is doing it too, keeping her life to herself, never even trying to share it with him.

Her thoughts are interrupted at the entrance to the souk. Even in the dark, she can read the words on the windshield of a car. Often kids will write in the dust, 'WASH ME PLEASE', or draw a crude Handala. What makes her stop and look is that the words are written in Hebrew: מוות לערבים, 'DEATH TO ARABS'. Maisoon shivers. She is used to seeing such hate-filled graffiti but never in her own neighbourhood. She quickly erases the words before hurrying home.

حيفا فراجمنتس

Majid remained in the garden for a long time after Maisoon left. When he finally walked inside, he found Layla in the salu, reading a book. He settled down beside her. "How could you, Layla?"

Layla looked up from her book, not comprehending.

"I thought we had an understanding about the past."

Still, Layla didn't understand.

"The letters, Layla, the letters! She found them!"

Layla sat up straight in her chair, "I see. And of course she came to you demanding answers?"

"She … she … that's not the point, Um Tayseer! The point is that you let her find them!" His voice was rising.

"Well, Abu Tayseer, how convenient for you to blame me. Let me remind you that you are the one who gave them to me without a word all those years ago. Remember? Without a word."

"Yes, but …" Majid's brow creased as he searched for words.

"But what, Abu Tayseer?"

"You were supposed to keep them away from Maisoon and Tayseer. It's my past. Layla, you had no right. She has no right!" He sank further into the soft recliner, realizing it was already too late.

"Then you should have burnt them, Majid." Layla said calmly.

"How could you even think that, Layla! Those papers are part of my history. Our history! The prison, resistance, everything. They're important!"

Layla took a deep breath, "Are you listening to yourself, Majid? Important to whom? Maisoon is your own blood. It's her history too. She has every right to know." She put the book on the table in front of her, and took her husband's hands in hers. "Majid, habibi, you have to face your past one day. You didn't burn those papers for a reason. Please, open your heart to Maisoon. If she came to you, then she needs it. Just as much as you do." There was fear in Majid's eyes but Layla felt the tension easing away from his hands. "Let's go to bed Abu Tayseer. Everything will be all right."

Majid stared at their hands. "How can you say that, Layla? Everything is wrong. Her quitting medical school … and … and …" It was hard for him to form the words. "She's going out with a Muslim! People are talking. And now this …" He sighed.

"Majid, it's her life, and she has the right to make her own decisions. She's no longer your little girl." She got up and stretched. "And I'm sure once you share your past with her, everything else will fall into place. Trust me. Now, can we go to bed?"

53

# 8

Christmas was approaching, though any signs of winter in Wadi Nisnas remained unnoticed. This was made up for by the countless red-blue-green-yellow-purple-sparkling-white lights hung in tangled splashes everywhere: on balkons, verandahs, windows, garden trees, strung across the narrow souk. Some were elaborately twisted on their cables into stars borrowed from the sky or just into some abstract forms. It was the time of year Maisoon cherished most. Christmas was, for her, a family tradition. This year, Layla decided on a humble family dinner. She told Maisoon and Tayseer they could invite guests, hinting that it was about time they met Ziyad.

"I'm not sure about it, Mais. It'll be awkward, especially with your father. And don't give me that look! It's your fault—hiding me away for so long." Ziyad was rolling a joint at the kitchen table.

"You don't have to come, you know. But I'd really like it if you did. It's nothing fancy, just a dinner. Tayseer is bringing two of his friends, and I thought to invite Shahd and … Amalia."

"What, you want to sit at the Eid table with your father, a Muslim boyfriend, our Shahd el-Falasteeniyya, and this Yahudiyya? You're not serious."

Three joints later, he was still laughing at the incongruity of the Christmas guests. "Ok, I'll come. At least I know it won't be boring.

But hey! I'm not bringing any presents for anyone!" A few minutes later, he was softly snoring on the diwan.

Maisoon covered him with a blanket and went back to work on her designs, but not before finishing the last joint. She gave in to the dizziness in her mind while slowly working the silver around the Labradorite translucent stone.

حيفا فراجمنتس

"Yalla, Shahd, we're already late!" Maisoon's voice comes through the balkon and reaches Shahd just as she steps out of the shower.

It's the night before Christmas Eve, and Shahd has managed to get away for a few days. She wants to feel the festive atmosphere in a place other than a refugee camp. "I wish you'd stop being so secretive and just tell me where we're going," Shahd squeezes her hair between her hands, dripping water onto the tiles.

"It's only ..." her sentence is cut short by the impatient horn of Tayseer's car.

"Yalla, seriously now, Shahd! Tayseer's waiting," she grabs a rumman-coloured scarf from the curtain of scarves. "Ten minutes. If you're not in the car by then, you can spend the evening here staring at Um Tawfiq's socks marching in the wind. And trust me, it's not an exciting sight. And don't forget to lock the door behind you."

Maisoon runs down the stairs, taking them two at a time, her shoulder bag flying behind her. A night of music, dancing and hasheesh. She gets into the car, slamming the door—the handle comes off in her hand—again. Tayseer laughs as she stares at the handle in disbelief.

"I can't believe you never learn, Mais."

She slaps his arm, frowns, and then hurls herself at him. He shrinks back, his back jamming into the car door handle, his face mock-horror. She hugs him tight. "I missed you," she plants a kiss on his nose. "Shahd's on her way down."

Tayseer frowns at his sister, then grabs the handle from her hand, and busies himself trying to fix it in place, his body stretching across Maisoon's lap.

Maisoon ruffles his wavy hair and smiles, "You know you're ruining my good name in the neighbourhood. Just think of the stories the old ladies will weave if anybody sees us in this ungodly position."

He laughs into the space between the door and her leg. "This Shahd of yours, does she smoke?" He feels her legs become rigid, her fingers in his hair stop mid-movement. He looks up at her in astonishment. "No! Don't tell me you have no idea!" He crawls backwards into his seat, straightens up and turns to her.

They stare at each other. Then burst into laughter. When Shahd finally gets into the car, Maisoon and Tayseer have a difficult time keeping a straight face.

حيفا فراجمنتس

Half an hour later, they cram into Isma'el's studio apartment, sitting on a diwan made up from old musty mattresses. Fairouz's bell of a voice is soft in the background.

"Always Fairouz at Isma'el's place," Maisoon whispers to Shahd.

On a coffee table—two bottles of cheap red wine. Next to them, the mythical small wooden box, inlaid with mother-of-pearl. Inside, the secrets of abandon. Shahd reaches out and picks up the box. Tayseer and Maisoon jerk their heads towards Isma'el and hold their breath. Nobody is allowed to touch the box. Isma'el watches Shahd.

Sensing she did something wrong, she looks up. "I was just ... it's just a beautiful box ... reminds me of the one my grandmother gave me when I was a girl." She quickly puts the box, unopened, back in its place.

Isma'el looked at Tayseer, who shrugs his shoulders. "Walla ..."

Isma'el winks at Maisoon, reaches for the box, and hands it back to Shahd. "You can look at it while I pour wine and Tayseer sets up the instruments. You! Maisoon! Don't look at me like that! Go and turn our dear Fairouz off. Time for a different kind of music."

Shahd sinks deeper into the diwan with the box in her hands. She looks at it closely—it's chipped in several places. She moves her finger over the antique clasp, and pushes it open. Slowly, she lifts the lid. Maisoon watches her silently, expectantly. First, it is curiosity, her eyes scanning the small objects scattered inside the box. Then, recognition. A pause. Eyes locking with Maisoon's. Then, slowly, a smile spreads across Shahd's face, and the room fills with the whoosh of three people exhaling. Shahd looks at them and bursts into laughter, "You thought I didn't suspect this? Mashallah!" she closes the box and puts it back on the coffee table. "I've never smoked ... this ..." indicating the box.

Isma'el raises his brows in delight. "But you're my guest now, and it would be just really, very rude to refuse the hospitality of my home."

An hour later, Maisoon is half sitting, half lying on the diwan. Her eyes glazing over, she is convinced she hears the souls of the two young men through their music. Their notes softly scribble onto her skin, Tayseer's durbakki racing Isma'el's oud. Her head slumps to the side, finding Shahd's shoulder. She closes her eyes and thinks of Ziyad. There is nothing solid for them, their worlds meet at an awkward angle. She pushes him from her mind and sinks further into the music.

Tayseer. Tapping his fingers on the oud as if it were a durbakki ... naked desire! You are angry—or do your feelings lose their names—their very significance—as they become sounds? Can you see the slivers of your music enter my body. Slowly, like a snake slithering down a tree. If it gets any slower it will become oh so painful. Then I—too—become music.

Her body converges with the sounds, in a dance of longing, yearning to find her roots in the liquid music that has become her body. Landless. Language-less. Reaching out for something to hold on to—anything to keep her from shrinking into a crumpled piece of a discarded history book. The music stops abruptly. Parts of Maisoon are still immersed in the sizzling sensation she always experiences after dancing to Tayseer's durbakki. Only his durbakki, combined with good hasheesh, can make her body move like that, detaching itself from her will. In the silence before Tayseer picks up another beat, the thought of the state's attempts at her—personal—permanent deletion by rewriting history books strikes her as Kafkaesque as she feels the hasheesh take her to a higher level. It terrifies her. She's filled with a desolate feeling that they want to delete her permanently—delete all signs of her memory. Of her ever being here. I am not wanted here—the place I call home. I am set to be deleted, simply and completely. Do they want to erase the history of a whole people? My language? The memory of my footprints? This dance of mine? Even that.

Another bottle of wine is opened and Isma'el rolls another joint. Passing it to Shahd, making sure his fingers don't touch hers, his voice is smoky, "Is it only me, or do you also see the music in colours?"

Shahd mumbles something which Maisoon doesn't really understand, about mountains and climbing up and then coming back down in the rain with the smell of grass everywhere.

Tomorrow, you will not be here. Tomorrow, Ziyad. Still, tonight—maybe … no … it's just this buzzing—all over on the insides of me. Already missing the scent of your hair—at the moment of inhaling it. Fresh laimoon. Yes. I see the music in colours. I feel your body scooting closer to mine, so soft, seductive. Closer now, and I feel your heartbeat. Just want to lie down and sleep. Tayseer take me home. No more colours. No more the scent of laimoon. Enough for one night.

ديفا فراجمنتس

Maisoon has planned a lazy day with Shahd, hanging out and catching up but on the morning of Christmas Eve she drifts in and out of sleep as the phone blasts into her dreams. When she finally crawls out of bed—she has no clear memory of how she got into it the night before—there are five missed calls and three short messages. She reads the messages first, all from Ziyad:

"what should I buy your parents?"

"call me when you wake up!" and

"where are you???"

She smiles at his panic. I thought you said no presents. She checks the missed calls—all from Amalia. Something urgent come up at the boutique? She dials Amalia's number first.

"Maisoon! I've been calling all morning!" her voice comes loud over the background noise, "I'm at the mall right now, and can't make up my mind. Does your mother like blue or green better?"

"What? I don't know. It depends." Of course sky blue. Mama's favourite colour.

"For Christmas, Maisoon! I'm getting your parents nice cotton bedding. Light blue or green?"

Oh. No. Not that colour in Mama's bedroom. Not from you. "Green, Amalia. Pale green." She only hears half of Amalia's thank you before the line goes dead. Your Star of David flag colour will not cover Mama in her sleep.

Waiting for the kahwa to boil, she dials Ziyad's number. His voice is not the rough one she expects, but rather smeared with unnatural sweetness.

"So ... I was thinking ... maybe I should get something for your parents after all ... you know, it's my first time ... and I want to make a good impression ..."

She smiles, "Uh-huh, and?"

"I thought you could ... you know, maybe ..."

"No," she cuts the sweetness in half, "don't even think about it, Ziyad! It's Christmas Eve, I've got stuff to do. You should have thought about it earlier. Good luck, and I'll see you in the evening. Send me a message when you're close by."

Before turning her mobile off to avoid any other Christmas crises, she calls her mother to see if she needs any help with dinner. Layla laughs into the phone, telling her that she is just about as helpful as Majid in the kitchen.

"You're a failed housewife Mais, accept it. But never blame me for it."

She walks into the salu with a tray of kahwa and two finjans, and looks down at what appears to be a heap of blankets. Snuggled inside is Shahd, her head turned towards the back of the diwan. Beautiful when you're sleeping. Maisoon sits on the cool floor next to Shahd. Caresses her long hair, moving it away from her face. The fresh laimoon scent is gone now; replaced by the smell of stale smoke. "Merry Christmas, habibti. Kahwa?"

Shahd's unfocused eyes are dim, her left cheek marked from pressing into the diwan. "Christmas presents trouble?" her words come out heavy with sleep, the voice not her own.

"No, nothing special. Hey, let's not get caught up in any Christmas dramas, let's do something fun. We can go down to the beach or walk up to Stella Maris. The weather is nice and cool."

They drink their kahwa on the balkon, enjoying the frantic shopping of women who have realized they are missing some ingredients for the festive dinner. Children run about—some on errands, while others seem intent on getting in the way, the jingle of their laughter bouncing off the Christmas decorations.

"We only have four Christian families in the mukhayyam," Shahd is leaning over the rail, following a girl of about four or five who is darting about. She is a blur of red, her flowing dress matches her shiny shoes. Two braids fly behind her trying to catch up as she disappears and reappears, finally slipping into a vegetable stall. Shahd sinks back into the wicker chair and sips her kahwa. It is her first Christmas where laughter isn't bound by barbed wire or cement walls. "Let's just stay home today. I want to feel all of this, breathe it in. I promised Ina'am and Shirin I'd tell them about it."

The day glides by lazily and in relative silence; the two women move through the apartment in comfortable intimacy. Maisoon spends most of the day on the diwan, working on some new sketches and reading Majid's writing in between cigarettes. Shahd moves between the diwan and the balkon, reading bits of Mahmoud Darwish between

60

running to see the source of laughter down in the souk and studying Maisoon's new sketches, offering feedback on the potential of transforming the two-dimensional pencil lines into pieces of jewellery.

In the late afternoon, Ziyad drops by with three halves of falafel, and they sit around the kitchen table to eat. His anxiety about meeting Maisoon's parents is detectable in his voice.

"Everything will be fine, Zeen. Khalti Layla is really a wonderful woman," Shahd tries to calm him with an artificially sweet tone.

"Huh? I'm more worried about Abu Tayseer than about Maisoon's mother," he growls back at her.

Shahd pulls out her claws, "Okay, worst case scenario: murder on family honour grounds."

At the last words, Maisoon winces. She gathers the paper bags from the falafel, bunches them into a ball and throws them at Ziyad. "Go and make us some shai." The look she gives him doesn't leave any opening for argument.

He knows that look. Maisoon is taking a moment to either withdraw or attack. He hopes she will withdraw but he can see she is being pulled in the other direction. When he is out of earshot, Maisoon says in a low voice, without looking at Shahd.

"I don't want to hear that expression again from you. Not in my apartment, Shahd."

Not comprehending, Shahd waits.

"Murder on family honour grounds. It's wrong, Shahd. That kind of thinking keeps us oppressed. It's not honour killing, Shahd. It's plain murder. The honour of my family isn't between my legs. It lies in leading a dignified, honest life. If I lead my life without causing harm to others, is that honour enough for you?" Her voice rises in anger as she looks Shahd in the eye, "If I'm honest and sincere, doesn't that count too? If my family are good people, is that honour enough? And if Tayseer has a girl and they make love, how come he's not sullying his family honour? Or does only the girl count? And why? I refuse this language. What I do with my body is my own business. Not my father's

61

business, and not my mother's. Not even Ziyad's. It's all my own." She looks away. When she looks at Shahd again, she sees that her eyes are glittering with tears. "I'm sorry, Shahd. I didn't mean to upset you, but this is how I feel about it. If I'm not married to Ziyad and we sleep together, do you really believe that this makes me a bad person?"

Shahd and Maisoon sit facing one another but avoiding eye contact. Ziyad walks in with the shai. Shahd straightens up, she wants to run out the door. She rubs her eyes and sees Maisoon do the same. Ziyad places the tray on the coffee table; the flat sound it makes breaks the silence. He leans over and puts his arm around Maisoon's shoulder, she doesn't soften until he whispers in her ear. He looks up at Shahd and smiles.

Shahd moves closer to Maisoon and squeezes her hand, "I'm sorry."

Maisoon sighs and kisses Shahd on the cheek.

"I should be going ... need to get ready for the evening. What time should I be here, Mais?"

"Around seven, I guess," she extends her neck for him to kiss it. "Oh, and don't worry about formal dress. Just come casual."

حيفا فراجمنتس

Layla moved effortlessly in and out of conversation with her guests. Majid put on his best crooked smile and was able to charm Amalia. Still, throughout the whole dinner, he struggled to look at the Muslim intruder sitting too close to his daughter, breathing her into him. But this was Christmas, and he was trying to put his disapproval aside for the evening. After dinner, they all gathered in the salu to open presents. Layla, as always, had just the right present for everyone.

But this year, it was one of Majid's gifts that took everybody's breath away. It was a small coffee table with Arabic calligraphy—the tiles were chipped here and there, but it only gave it more charm and authenticity. The wood was a beautiful dark wine colour. When Majid read out Amalia's name on the tag, she almost choked on her drink.

"Oh, no. I can't accept this, Abu Tayseer." She looked at Maisoon, who only shrugged in response.

"Can't help you here, Amalia. It's Baba's coffee table."

Sensing the Jewish woman's awkwardness, Layla got up from her chair and went to join Amalia on the sofa while the others continued with the exchanging of gifts. "It's alright, Amalia. It's his choice. For us, Christmas is not about religion. It's about closeness and ..." she moved closer and lowered her voice, "and about love." Layla placed her hand over Amalia's fragile white hand. "Look. I didn't know he was giving this to you tonight. It's been in his family for years. When his father died, his mother gave it to him. It's the one piece of furniture he loves in this house. It's his way of saying thank you." She reached for Amalia's other hand and whispered, "Please accept it." Her hands were warm, Amalia's cool. Tears glistened in Amalia's eyes as she nodded her head.

When Ziyad stepped out into the now dark garden to smoke, Majid followed him. He put a cigarette in his mouth and when Ziyad saw he was searching his pockets for a lighter, he offered the older man a light.

"Shukran," Majid said.

They stood in the dark, smoking in silence. When Ziyad finished his cigarette and turned to go back in, Majid put his arm on his shoulder. He would make an effort to get to know Ziyad.

"Maisoon tells me you completed architecture studies at the Technion."

"Yes, but you know how the employment market is in this place ... I'm too dark for any Jewish companies, and too proud to accept a job that my father fixed for me. So I work for a cell-phone company for now."

"Yes, I know what you're talking about. But you shouldn't lose hope."

Majid offered Ziyad a cigarette from his pack, and they continued to talk about the economy, both avoiding more personal topics. A laugh reached them from inside, and both men looked back through the window. Majid caught Maisoon's eyes; they were twinkling. "Come on, let's go back in. We don't want to miss the dessert now, do we?"

In the kitchen, Shahd was helping Layla with the dessert. Tayseer and his two friends were playing cards in the salu, and Amalia and Maisoon were talking in hushed tones about some business. Ziyad joined the game of cards, and Majid settled in a recliner. When Amalia saw him looking in the direction of his daughter, she excused herself, "I'm going to the kitchen to check on the progress of that dessert. They might need another hand."

Maisoon got up, fumbled in her bag for her pack of cigarettes and walked out to the garden. Majid followed her.

"You look beautiful tonight." He sat down next to her. "And happy," he admitted.

"I am happy, Baba. And I appreciate you being nice to Ziyad," Maisoon smiled at her father.

"But you know, people are talking ... they see him coming to your apartment at all hours of the day and night and it's just ... it's not right. You know what I mean." He tried to keep his voice low and stay calm, it was Christmas after all and he had promised Layla not to get into it with Maisoon. At least not tonight. But he couldn't help himself. "When I let you move into grandfather's house, it never crossed my mind that you would ..." he sighed. "I mean ... why can't you just find yourself a good young educated Christian man? And you should also start thinking about getting married."

Maisoon had known that this would come at some point, but she never imagined it would come in such a bold form. "So let me get this straight. Is this about me having a Muslim partner or the fact that he spends the night at my place and the whole neighbourhood knows about it? What is it that bothers you exactly, Baba?" Her voice was a whispering rage. "Baba, wake up! We're in the twenty-first century."

"Can you at least be more discreet?"

"Why? Baba, I'm no different from the neighbours' daughters who tell their parents they're going to sleep over at a girlfriend's house or make up any other excuse and then go out and spend the night in the Galilee in some cabin with their boyfriends. The only difference is that I don't go sneaking around."

Majid shifted and looked out into the garden, unsure who was right or wrong.

Maisoon stared at the house, Layla, Shahd and Amalia were already in the salu with the dessert, and the men were getting up from the game of cards to sit at the large dining table. She stood up, put her hand on her father's shoulder, and said. "I refuse to live a lie. Now let's go have Mama's dessert before Tayseer and his friends devour it all."

# 9

ذ The short winter months passed through Haifa without much
notice. Maisoon spent her days working on new jewellery pieces
for the boutique, and reading and rereading Majid's history,
trying to unravel it all so that she had a beginning, a middle and end,
but failing over and over. Starting from a different piece each time.
Ziyad disrupted her only a few times, he was spending the whole winter
in the village, doing his family duty. His mother had fallen seriously ill
and he was the only unmarried son. Shahd came for the weekend every
two or three weeks, depending on the weather and the availability of
Mansour.

Maisoon worried about her, knowing that she was travelling through
the no-go area and becoming increasingly careless. Miraculously, the
only damage was to her boots and Maisoon's floor from the caked mud.
They would spend the weekends talking, the cold nights providing
fertile ground for closeness and intimacy. By the time spring came,
Shahd's clothes were taking up several shelves in Maisoon's closet, her
toothbrush a permanent resident in the bathroom. When Shahd wasn't
around, Maisoon found herself restless, increasingly missing her
presence and her warmth which would fill the apartment.

حيفا فراجمنتس

"You look so handsome in those photographs, Baba."

They are sitting in the garden again, their usual spot in the corner. Layla has disappeared, making up a lame excuse about Um Suleiman not feeling well, sensing that her daughter needs some time alone with Majid. Maisoon came armed with a few photographs, hoping they would tempt her father to open up. She doesn't dare ask about his writing or Asmahan yet. Majid takes a photo of himself and studies it. This time, he decides to give Maisoon what she wants and soon the words are spilling from him like Nisan's rain.

"The first play I wrote was in high school. I remember it was the end of the year, and we wanted to put on something political, to express our protest at the military rule, the oppression and the political persecutions. We were so proud of ourselves, the actors performing with such zeal. At the end of the play, my father practically dragged me home. He was furious, I didn't understand until years later that his rage hid his fear. You have to remember, those years were very unstable, and there was so much confusion among my father's generation about everything: loyalties, identities, politics, forced detachment from the rest of our people. A lot of young people were engaged in passionate resistance—public and underground. But there were also many who were collaborating with the mukhabarat. It was difficult to know your friends from your enemies. It took me years to understand my father's fear for his family's safety … and to forgive him.

"Back home he tried to beat the writing out of my bones. And I let him think he had succeeded. But I continued to write plays with even more zeal and passion than before. Later I couldn't remember if I was doing it because I loved it or just to spite my father. It became an obsession, just knowing that I was able to do it. Of course it eventually blew up in my face … you see I had the nerve to enrol in the department of theatre at the university. The whole time my father thought I was studying law. Psh! I can't believe he didn't see right through me, because I practically flaunted it in front of him. I think I wanted him to know. But then, when he found out from a letter that

67

arrived home from the university, some kind of an invitation to a play, I thought my life was over right then and there. You know what he did? He actually went to the university and informed them that his son would no longer be a theatre student. But he didn't stop there. He marched right up to the department of law and enrolled me for the following semester. Paid the whole year's tuition up front, so that was the end of university for me. Of course I didn't study law. Though looking back, I think I could have been a great lawyer! But my father was not going to decide for me. I had to fight and argue with him for a whole month before he let go. He was very stubborn—sometimes you and Tayseer remind me of him with your stubbornness. He tried to pull strings, telling me that anything else I studied I'd have to pay for myself. And so I did. I took two years off to work and save. And then I enrolled in economics studies … and that was the end of it."

He lights a cigarette, hands it to Maisoon and lights another one for himself. It's a sign that he's finished talking for tonight. It was more than Maisoon had hoped to get out of him.

She feels triumphant—until she begins to recall her father's words. What she has now is another piece of the story, but it's still far from being complete. There are too many details forgotten—or left out intentionally. Where does his poetry writing fit in? Did he completely abandon writing plays when his father found out? And what about Asmahan? He didn't mention her at all. But at least I got a few good bits out of him. Majid disobeying his own father. And a student of theatre! Oh Tayseer, can't wait for you to find out!

68

# 10



Maisoon and Shahd burst into Amalia's Jewellery. A woman in her early forties, catching the rising-falling rhythm of the Arabic words, smiled nervously at the two women and bent her head back over the showcase.

"Oh, Irit! You're lucky, here's the designer." Amalia smiled at her customer. "Maisoon, you saved me. Irit would like to know the name of this stone."

Maisoon looked at the necklace without moving from where she stood. "That's Larimar, beautiful colour." She was watching the woman trying it on, looking at her blue eyes reflected in the mirror. "Hmm. No. I'm sorry, but this stone isn't for you."

Amalia glanced at Maisoon but remained silent.

"It's one of my favourites, but look how pale it makes your eyes look. Let's see," she scanned the necklaces in similar designs, glancing every now and then at the waiting woman's face. "Here, this will bring out the spark in your eyes. Jade."

The woman put the necklace on and looked in the mirror, "I see. I guess you're right. But I don't like the design of this one." She turned and picked up the Larimar necklace again.

"No problem. You like this design? I can make you one just like it, with the Jade. I can have it ready for you in about two weeks."

Amalia stepped in, "But you know, because it's made on order, there will be an extra charge." Maisoon shot her a look, but didn't say a word.

Fifteen minutes later, they were seated outside the boutique, drinking na'ana shai at the table Maisoon had set up for herself under the awning.

"Anyway," Maisoon was saying in between drags of bluish smoke, "I was visiting Shahd's family last weekend, and you know, it was just amazing. There were three women at their house with Um Loai, all busy stitching these beautiful coin purses, bags, tablecloths. There was such intimacy between them."

Turning to Shahd, Amalia's business mind snapped into action, "You have samples?" She asked Shahd in English, since that was the only language they both knew.

"Not really ... just my purse and bag. My mother made these."

Amalia took the purse in her hands and studied it. "Maisoon, what do you say? We can string the bags against the wall and display some of the purses and tablecloths on a couple of shelves."

Maisoon, shocked at Amalia's ignorance, only nodded in silence, not knowing how to tell Amalia that it was a bit more complicated than that.

"I ... I don't think that would work ..." Shahd said, a bit confused.

"Of course it will work. Why wouldn't it?" Amalia was getting all worked up.

Sensing Shahd's discomfort, Maisoon intervened, "It's just that ... well, I'm not sure they would want to do business with ..."

"Israelis." Shahd finished Maisoon's sentence, seeing the awkward position her friend was in.

"But ... I don't understand ..."

"Amalia," Maisoon lit another cigarette. "Shahd doesn't know Hebrew because she's from a refugee camp. In the occupied West Bank." She let the words sink in.

Shahd was surprised by the Yahudiyya's ignorance and explained to her about her refugee camp's non-violent resistance to the Occupation.

70

The whole community was boycotting anything and everything that smelled Israeli. The price was heavy—paid mainly by the women and children who bore the brunt. But this was what Palestinian sumud was all about, after all. Seeing the men losing hope with each sunset, the women had begun to organize. Small groups sprouted in kitchens, where the women stitched and devised ways to sell the handcrafts: hand-stitched traditional dresses, scarves, purses, bags, and home-made olive oil and soap all loaded onto the back of Abu Hamza's dilapidated truck and taken to Ramallah's souk through the back roads. Two of the refugee camp's young women took charge of selling in the unforgiving souk, while two older women took their wares to the expensive tourist arts and crafts shops. It took them several weeks and a great deal of negotiation to make a deal with the owner of one of the shops. The deal was pathetic, but they were in no position to stand their ground. So now, Abu Hamza made a trip once a month to Ramallah, his truck loaded to bursting, returning in the evening with a thin envelope containing the meagre amount of money. After deducting the gas for the round trip and the cost of the raw materials, the women were left with a pitiful amount. But they continued to stitch and sew, for they had no other choice but sumud.

Amalia listened in a daze. This was happening so close yet a world away from her own comfortable life.

Maisoon saw her struggling to make sense of it all and spoke up, "Amalia, just forget about it. Business is done differently there. You don't need to understand all the reasons now, but you have to respect their ways."

Leaving the boutique, Maisoon wondered whether she'd done the right thing by selling to a Jewish boutique. She thought of Tal E-Zeitun and the people she'd met there. Would they think she was practising Normalization of the Occupation by working for a Yahudiyya? Life was complicated enough living in a mixed city. It would be practically impossible to stop every time she had an interaction with a Jew and ask herself if it was Normalization or not.

Late in the evening, Maisoon walked the short distance from her apartment to her parents' house while Shahd stayed at the apartment reading a book. She found Majid in his pyjamas already, watching the evening news.

"Salam, Baba," she said as she dropped onto the couch next to him.

"I know that face. You want something, so spill it out and save us the puppy looks."

Maisoon couldn't tell whether or not he was in a good mood. "I just need to borrow the car tomorrow so I can take Shahd back to the mukhayyam."

Majid now switched his focus from the news to his daughter. "I see you and Shahd have become very close friends. It's nice, really, but you have to understand something, Mais. It's not about you and Shahd. It's much bigger than that."

"What do you mean, Baba?" Maisoon straightened up.

"They're not like us. What's there not to understand?"

"We're the same people, on both sides of the green line. It's an artificial division, it's not real."

"No, Mais. See, this is where you're wrong. We were divided into isolated geographical areas, and time has changed us. Look at yourself. Look at your home, at the way you live. We are westernized. They are not. There's no longer a collective 'we'. Can't you see it?" He sounded exasperated, as if trying to explain something to a stubborn child.

"But these differences are a result of the Occupation, Baba. We're still part of the same people," Maisoon heard herself repeating a cliché … but then she genuinely believed it.

"We have grown apart," Majid squished his cigarette into the ashtray, "and that's a fact you can't argue with. The keys to the car are on the hook in the hallway. Oh, and do me a favour and be careful out there. I don't have the energy to deal with it if you get yourself arrested."

She opened the door but stopped and walked back to the sofa. "You know something, Baba? I really don't get it. What is it in essence that makes us different? Why can't you feel that you belong?"

72

Majid flicked the TV off and looked straight into his daughter's eyes. "Maisoon, take a look at your own life. Your struggles are nothing like theirs. To live in a country that doesn't have your name on its flag. To keep having to spell out your name to clerks. To be looked at with hatred whenever you say something in a language that is not yours. To read signs in a language you didn't read at home. To be reminded that this land, the land your family tilled for hundreds of years, is not yours any more. To feel exiled in your own land. Not wanted. These are our struggles.

"Now go to the mukhayyam tomorrow and see how that holds up to Um Loai's daily life."

حيهّا فراجمنتس

On entering the mukhayyam neighbourhood the following day, Maisoon was welcomed by the children. "The Heifawiya is here"—the woman from Haifa is here—echoed from rooftop to rooftop and the patter of bare feet followed. Twenty pairs of small, warm hands grabbed at her, hugging her or bouncing up and down to tell her something. They smelled of earth and sun. Maisoon caught snatches of questions and adventures yelled at her. Once the kids' energy had peaked, she crouched down and opened her backpack, pulling out books, crayons, and educational games. Olive-coloured hands quickly snatched them up.

Over lunch, Shahd told her mother about Haifa, "You should have seen the expression on the Yahudiyya's face when she discovered I was from the other side of her world, Mama. She had no idea. I actually had to spell things out to her."

"What Yahudiyya?" Um Loai looked at Maisoon with surprise.

Until now, Maisoon had avoided talking about her work with Um Loai, not knowing how the older woman would accept the fact she worked for a Jewish woman. Although Um Loai didn't say anything, but only nodded, Maisoon felt she was being silently accused of working for—collaborating with!—a Yahudiyya.

She was surprised when, before leaving, Um Loai handed her a small leather pouch full of authentic Palestinian coins—all of them with holes in their middle. "When the time is right, your heart will know what to do with them."

On the way back to Haifa, Maisoon tried to figure out Um Loai. Um Loai's food tasted exactly like her own mother's, the extra finjan was always there, the hospitality—more pronounced at Um Loai's house, maybe out of a desperate groping for some sense of normality. These, to Maisoon, seemed the essence of what united them. But there was so much more to it. New values adopted under inhuman conditions, desperate actions of sumud, daily negotiations that all too often robbed the women of their dignity. The men who once worked twelve, fifteen or sixteen hours a day in construction, making an honest living, now unemployed, bent low to the ground, unable to look their wives in the eye as they dropped the sack of rice from the foreign aid agency at their feet. She was at once humbled and awed at the steadfastness and unwavering strength of this woman.

Her own battles for a normal existence—the things Majid told her the night before—seemed all of a sudden insignificant compared to those of Um Loai's and the rest of the camp's women. Hers were battles of privilege; the battles of Tal E-Zeitun women were battles of survival. She was beginning to understand what her father meant when he said they'd grown apart.

## 11

In her attempt to reconcile these different worlds, Maisoon invited Layla to join her on one of her trips to Tal E-Zeitun. But Majid interfered. It isn't safe these days. It took her two weeks to convince him to let Layla go. True, theirs was a very liberal home; Layla was free to go where she pleased, but her freedom only stretched as far as the green line. When he finally agreed, Maisoon hugged him.

On their way to the mukhayyam, Maisoon kept glancing at Layla, looking for signs of distress, but none appeared on the older woman's face. When she asked her mother how she felt, Layla replied, "You forget that I used to do my weekly shopping in Jenin back then. Back before all this insanity intensified and tore us even farther apart." Her voice was veiled in sadness.

Maisoon wound down her window, the wind whipped her hair around her face. The rise and fall of the dry land hardly registered with her, she was thinking of her father and wondering when he surrendered. She turned to her mother, "Tell me the story of how you and Baba met." She had heard it before but sensed there were important parts left out. She wanted to hear it again, to see how it fitted in with what she'd learned about her father. Writing, prison, Asmahan.

"I met your father in the autumn of 1976. It was a difficult year for all of us here, after the March 30th first Land Day. We took to the streets enraged about the expropriation of our land for the sake of Judaization of the Galilee."

Maisoon inhaled impatiently, "Mama, I know the story of the Land Day."

"Yes, habibti, but what you don't know is that I had been engaged to be married before I met your father," Layla said.

Maisoon eased her foot off the gas, taking in this unexpected piece of new information.

"My fiancé was shot dead at the demonstration. I was devastated, and couldn't function for months. I thought my life had come to an end. I think it was my mother's idea for me to move away from all the places that constantly reminded me of him, and so I moved in with my widowed aunt in Haifa. At first I would just walk the streets of this new city, getting the feel of it. I felt so lost, didn't have any friends, no job, and the future was unclear. Then one day, as I was walking around in Hadar, I passed a bank. It was then I realized I wanted to stay in Haifa. I couldn't go back, not to all those memories. So I walked in and decided to transfer my account to this bank in Haifa.

"His dark looks betrayed his blood, but still I wasn't sure, so I came closer and read his name tag. May I interrupt? I said. He looked up from the paperwork in front of him, and frowned at me. Tfaddali. All his movements were very formal and distant. For twenty minutes, the time it took to open a bank account, I watched the sadness in his eyes. When we finished, I got up to leave, paused, and turned back to him. He was already immersed again in his paperwork, so I asked him if he knew where I could get a good falafel. Majid looked up at me, quite surprised, not understanding the hint. Wadi Nisnas, of course. The best falafel in Haifa. I didn't thank him, and just stood there, waiting. When he saw I hadn't moved, he added it's really close, you just go down a couple of streets from here ... I was still looking at him, waiting, now with a defiant smile. It was then that something in him snapped back to life. Tayyeb, tayyeb! You are a stubborn young lady. We close in half an hour.

76

"There were embers in his eyes, left over from a fire extinguished long ago. I knew I would never be able to make that fire rage again. But I slowly worked up a small and steady camp-fire, one you can keep going without it devouring the whole forest. We both knew we could never compete with what each of us had lost. Yet it was this grief that made our love possible. In the beginning, we were two half-humans making less than a whole. Habibti ... I don't know what words to use about what went on between your father and me. But I know his love for me is a love that grew out of grief. I don't resent him for it ... how could I ... when my own love for him grew out of mourning. We used to talk about the people we'd lost—they actually came back to life and fed on our love for a while there ... until they saw that we were doing fine on our own, and then they slowly receded back into the shadows, leaving us to ourselves. In this place, where we are forever reminded of what we've lost, this is the only possible way for love to make a home in your heart. I don't think it's a compromise, because Allah knows how much I love your father. Am I making any sense to you, Mais?"

Maisoon looked across at her mother, they were nearing the check-point. Yes, she was making sense in a twisted way. But she couldn't afford to start thinking about it now. They had kids with machine guns to deal with.

حيفا فراجمنتس

As they were nearing the mukhayyam, Maisoon was surprised to see her mother partly cover her hair with a pale green scarf. "Mama ... what ..."

"It's all right, habibti. It's just a small gesture of respect. A thing of my generation. Yalla, let's go."

The children, seeing Maisoon in the company of an older woman, faltered. They approached the two women in small, hesitating steps, but when they saw Maisoon bend over her backpack, they scrambled towards her, leaving Layla stunned into a smile.

"Welcome, welcome, what an honour! Um Tayseer tfaddali my home is your home." Um Loai, though unprepared by Shahd for this visit, didn't lose any of her grace. "Shahd, put on the kettle of shai, and don't forget the fresh na'ana!" her strong voice reverberated in the small house. "Abu Loai! Put on your bantaloon and come. Um Tayseer is here!"

That afternoon, Maisoon realized how little she knew her own mother. It was the first time also for her to learn Um Loai's name. I've been visiting this family for months, and it never crossed my mind to ask for Um Loai's name! And here was Layla, calling the other woman Suhad only five minutes after arriving. She watched the two women sitting at the kitchen table, laughing without restraint, telling stories, getting to know each other. Maisoon could tell that Layla felt at home and seemed unconcerned about being accepted.

Before heading back home, Suhad made Layla promise to come visit again soon. "Because it's so much easier for you to cross the hajez than me ..." Suhad added with sadness.

When the two women hugged, Shahd and Maisoon smiled at each other.

It was evening when they arrived back home. They had just settled with their shai in the salu when Majid walked in from the bathroom, a dark green towel wrapped around his big body. "By the smirks on your faces I can see the two of you had a good time today." He stood at the entrance to the salu, just on the edge of the carpet, "Let me just get dressed, and I'll join you for some of that shai."

"Baba, Um Loai invited us all next week for dinner," Maisoon couldn't hold back her excitement, "of course that also means you. She'd love to meet you."

Majid froze in his tracks, a perplexed look on his face which quickly changed to horror then fury. "No!"

Layla got up to face him. "Abu Tayseer, it's only an invitation to dinner. You knew what could happen when you let me go, Majid." Her voice was flat but Maisoon sensed a quiver in it.

Majid stared at her, his fury only growing bigger in his eyes, expanding into his whole body, making him look taller. He breathed in, breathed out. His next words were spoken in the calm of a steady rain on a windless day. "I will not have this in my house. If this daughter of yours wants to get into trouble with the mukhabarat, she can do it by herself. I paid with parts of my life. No. You will not drag me back there! I don't want to hear one more word about it. Not in my house."

Layla didn't move, her body a shield. "Not in your house, Majid? I would like to remind you that I live here too. This is my house too. We will not put you in danger. But you know what? I really did enjoy my time at the mukhayyam today with Um Loai's family and I would like to visit again."

Majid looked at his soft-spoken wife, the woman who never did anything against his will.

"You do remember that even though I'm your wife I am a free woman. Or have you forgotten that, too?" Layla turned her back on Majid and was relieved when she heard him walk away.

حيفا فراجمنتس

That evening, Maisoon declined Ziyad's offer of hasheesh. So much in one day; she needed time to take it all in. She tried to fit in the Majid of today with the soft Majid of Layla's story as she recalled what her mother had said about love growing out of grief. Yes, she could understand how it could be. Wasn't her own love—if she could define it as that—for Ziyad based on similarly twisted emotions? Hers wasn't out of grief though; it was born of pain, anger and frustration.

Her father's fury though, she thought was groundless. Her family was not important enough for the mukhabarat. So many Palestinian citizens of Israel travelled to the occupied West Bank on a regular basis, and nothing ever happened to them. But then there were also those who had been persecuted and even imprisoned for acts more trivial than visiting friends and family beyond the wall.

# 12

Majid cannot sleep. His past is closing in on him. Maisoon has succeeded in bringing up all those long buried emotions. In the morning he takes off for Al-Quds. He is tired of it all, having given up hope and faith years ago, when he saw that the struggle over home was turning into a religious war. So many arguments over this one word. Al-Quds. Almost everybody has this conflict figured out all wrong. No, there is no room for any incongruence—not in the newspapers, not in people's minds. They only want to know the basics—who's against whom and over what so that they can look smart.

Driving up the mountainous road leading to Al-Quds, Majid rolls down the car window to feel the drop in temperature. The city has changed so much, yet it remains the same. He becomes lost in the maze of new roads, finds his way again, and reaches his destination, parks his car just outside the old city.

He walks in through Damascus Gate, known in Arabic as Bab Al-Amoud. Suddenly, the air feels thicker, denser, as if there is not enough to go around. He inhales the intensity of it. He notices more soldiers to one square space, more machine guns in that same space. The more soldiers and guns he sees, the less secure he feels.

He spends most of the day walking through the souk and the alleys of the old city, breathing in the sights. Nineteen-year-old soldiers harassing young boys of no more than twelve or thirteen, bullying them with the butts of their machine guns in dark corners of the souk. Small boys selling lighters and cheap razors. Groups of ultraorthodox Jews hurrying past, oblivious to their surroundings. The smell of shawarma meat wafting from a corner place. Veiled women buying fruit and vegetables. White tourists sprinkled through, shopping for souvenirs from this Holy Land. A woman balancing a large basket on her head. An improvised stand with a boy of about fifteen selling freshly squeezed rumman juice. His face is dark from the sizzling Middle Eastern sun, his light brown eyes shimmering, catching the blood red of the fruit. His white tanktop in gleaming contrast to his olive skin, jeans smeared with dapples of various shades of rumman colour—some fresh, others old— like the cloth a painter cleans a brush on before dipping it into another colour.

Majid pauses at the side of the stand, watching a tourist in her late thirties trying to barter down the price of a cup of the paradise drink. The young boy smiles politely, refusing to lower the price. The woman's brow creases, but she buys the drink anyway, not wanting to appear stingy. She walks away taking sips as she reunites with her friends.

"A cold rumman drink, muallem? Only ten shekels for a taste of paradise." The boy is squeezing a fresh fruit into a tin cup with one hand, holding a sieve over it with the other so that the juice dripping into the cup is pure.

Majid smiles back at the boy as he pays for his drink and continues his wandering through the old city.

Somehow he ends up at the Wailing Wall, and reaches Al Aqsa Mosque. He stands outside and watches people going in. We're all prisoners of propaganda. The sword of religion was handed to us falsely and we are fighting the great war of religion. We've forgotten history. There will be no justice until we realize this big lie. But until then we're bound to Al-Quds with chains of iron. We are not the keepers of Islam. This is a struggle over home. Religion has nothing to do with it.

This thought takes him back to Maisoon. She is dealing with it on such a different level. Picking up young boys and girls from the

81

checkpoints for medical treatment. Such futile tasks, with no end in sight. Just one child at a time. What's the point? It strengthens the Occupation. It gives people just enough space to breathe, but nothing beyond that. Instead of dealing with the roots of it, Maisoon is patching up individual bruises. But is that so wrong? It is something, and it is so much more than him doing nothing. He moves closer to the mosque and looks at the devout passing into the cool interior, their faces a mask of religious certainty. He wonders how religious Ziyad's family are and his face flushes. He is not only being dishonest to his family, he is being dishonest to Asmahan and the memory of their love.

It is dusk when he heads back north, towards home. Al-Quds disappears from his rear-view mirror but he feels it in his lungs. He reaches for the dial and turns on the radio, fiddling until he finds an Arabic station. The rest of the way home he hums along to the familiar tunes.

# 13

the connection to the body
writing script on the body
though pencil—it will not be erased
to remember always—all that was
the comfort of your body—the smile of you
under my skin—memory crawls—slowly

I demand my memories back
reverse the flow of my blood
retrace my steps—
before pain, grief, agony
a time when sunflowers made me smile
a time when butterflies landed in my palms
you were there to cup them in your hands
if I try hard enough, I can still remember—
brush of the butterfly's breath on my arm
that memory of you—
I take to the grave.

Maisoon reread the lines several times aloud, tasting the words on her tongue. Then imagining her father writing them. Did he write them to Asmahan while they were lying under an olive tree? Or did he write them when he was alone, in some dark corner? The paper was brown at the edges, the ink fading blue. The piece wasn't dated, but she figured it must have been well after prison. It seemed as if he were regretting the end of their love, yet his anger was still there.

She put the sheet of paper on her chest, her hands holding it there, and lifted her head. "I'm so tired, Ziyad. Of everything." They were in Maisoon's apartment, the retreating day taking away the heat with it. Maisoon was lying down on the diwan, her bare feet propped up on Ziyad's knees for a massage.

"Tayyeb, what's the problem? Just let go. You know you can't fix it, so why bother? I mean, I don't bother with it too much. It's got nothing to do with me. Just live your life like a normal person."

"See! This is exactly what I mean. I just don't understand you. How can you say such nonsense? It has everything to do with you. And me. You're either ignorant or you are closing your mind."

He reached for a pack of cigarettes and kicked back; was it the flicker of sadness she glimpsed in his eyes? His face was drawn in a silent mask.

"How could you detach yourself from it all? Say something! Don't you care about where this place is heading?" She felt her heart beat faster.

And still he was calm, slowly dragging on his cigarette, looking out past the balkon to a distant spot beyond the souk. "You are so smart, Mais. But sometimes you can be really stupid, you know? How can you think that I care nothing about this place? This is my history in the making too. But not everybody's like you. Not everybody needs to have their actions acknowledged all the time. And you know something else? You revel in the misery—it's what keeps you alive. It fills you up and drugs you to the bone. It's what gets you through the day. Not me. I want to live my life. I want to build something for myself, something small that can get me through this life. But I'm not indifferent to what's happening. I live it all just as much as you do. It affects me just the same. I'm tired too, Mais."

His voice trailed off for a moment, before gathering more force. "You're so full of it that you don't—can't—see that other people deal with it too. It's just that we each have our own way of handling it. I'm not like you, Mais. I face it on a completely different level. Am I bothered by the fact that I get searched wherever I go? Do I give a shit that the boy next to me on the bus carries a machine gun? Does it not get to me when I hear on the news that some small girl was shot dead because she was suspected of being a terrorist?"

She could see the vein on his left temple bulging now.

"Yes, Mais. I'm aware of what goes on. I live here too! But I can't let it dictate my whole existence. I try to keep it at a safe distance. It's the only way for some sanity in this place. For me, at least."

It was the first time Maisoon had heard him speak so openly about his feelings. Until now, there had been a silent pact between them, but it seemed that it had just been broken. But Ziyad slipped back into his protective cocoon, and busied himself with making a joint.

حيفا فراجمنتس

A few drags of hasheesh tonight—not marijuana like always—and she feels her heavy body slipping out of her and—in thin slices—sliding down towards the sheets, detaching itself from her in the process. Her body falls away, into the dim, clinging fragrance of white desire.

Giving up the possession of her body to Ziyad, knowing he will be gentle as he takes her to a whole new level. He is entranced by her passivity, her inability to control her desire for him. They are wrapped in their heat. The transition to this sublevel of elusive being is smooth, with its seductivity brushing against her, lightly breathing into her body.

Only when she abandons herself, the moment the silky waters of orgasm leave her body, spilling out in a wild eruption—only then does he start taking in the pleasure. He waits, holding back his outburst, not releasing until he feels her body has given up. He then enters her with passion.

Later, as they lie side by side, their fingers intertwined, and as she curls into his body, he whispers into her hair, "Alhamdulillah for the invention of marijuana and hasheesh. For only when you're under their influence do you become tame. Only then can I claim you as mine."

Ziyad holds on to her as she leaves him awake alone, stroking her hair. It is very rare that she falls asleep before him, and he takes the opportunity to study her face in the dim light of the burning candle. Asleep, her face is softer, the shadows that haunt her every waking moment have receded. He shifts his gaze to the candle, and lets his mind wander back to Maisoon's accusations earlier. It isn't true that he is detached from it all. How could she even think that? But then how could she think otherwise, when he doesn't dare share what happened on that fateful bus ride back in the spring of 2003? But he couldn't let her in on that horror, no way ...

The twenty-year-old Mahmoud Kawasme would come to him at night, haunting his dreams, driving them out only to be replaced by nightmarish screams and howls of anguish. He could never let Maisoon into his nightmares, just as he knew that she kept parts of her own pain to herself. But the untold grief would spill out of them both when they made love, just like tonight. Breaking free from their bodies and leaving them spent.

He wasn't good at reading people's faces. Not that he ever made an effort. He was waiting for the 37 bus in Hadar. He remembers that he'd been annoyed because he was late for his shift in the computer lab. The racket of a group of four teenage boys, all with McDonald's ice-creams, further irritated him. Later that day, he would try and re-construct their faces, trying to figure out if any of those kids had finished their ice-cream. The last one of their life.

It was March. The time of year Maisoon loved most. The weather played tricks on people. The result—people walking down the street in jackets and heavy sweaters, greeted by others in short sleeves and tanktops.

86

The boys at the bus stop were talking in hushed tones as two girls approached and stood to the side, schoolbags flung carelessly at their feet, throwing shy glances every now and then at the boys. Was one of them the twelve-year-old Qamar, who would never make it home from school, and never get to do her homework?

It seemed like the bus would never come. He looked at his watch—fifteen minutes. He'd give it five more and then catch a taxi. It was then that he looked to his left and saw him standing off to the side, a loner. Later he would learn his name: Mahmoud Kawasme. His eyes were darting edgily, though the rest of his face gave off extreme calmness. A university student, Ziyad thought, by the bulging backpack on his shoulder, the bloodshot eyes and the haggard body.

The bus finally arrived. Ziyad waited for the two girls and one of the boys with the ice-cream to get on the bus, and glanced back at the student. He was still standing to the side, unmoving. Just as the bus was about to pull out of the station, he approached in fast strides, as if suddenly remembering something, got on the bus as an afterthought and, after quickly scanning the bus, positioned himself close to the back door. Ziyad sat towards the end, where he knew he wouldn't have to get up to let any grey-haired old ladies sit.

For months after the bombing, he would go over and over these moments. Hard as he tried, he could never see Qamar on the bus. Was she the girl who got on the bus with her girlfriend? Where did she sit? Was she standing next to Mahmoud Kawasme or was she sitting close to Ziyad? There was one thing he would strain to forget but which kept creeping back into his mind. Those numbered seconds Mahmoud had his eyes locked on his. The small dark eyes spelt death. But they were also telling him to get the hell off the bus—immediately. That is, if he wanted to live. Ziyad's brain had stopped working. The only thing it did was send rapid instructions down his legs to get off the bus. And he did. Seconds later, the earth shook. Ziyad remembered the deathly, stony silence after the blast. Birds stopped their song. People froze. Then, jhannam. Animal-like howls. He was running in delirium, gasping for air. He didn't understand why he was running. He just knew he had to. The stench of burnt flesh filled his lungs.

In his nightmares, he runs into the thick, black smoke. His lungs drink in the almost fluid substance and he begins to choke. And then— nothingness. Sometimes Mahmoud comes to him in other forms, surprising him with a nargila. But it was only months later that the dreams came, after he'd discovered that Mahmoud, at twenty, had been a student of computer science. He invites him for a smoke of apple m'assal. They sit together, amid the rubble of what used to be Mahmoud's family home and smoke. And every time, Ziyad tries to ask him why ... but the words turn into ash inside his mouth.

# 14

Ziyad is dreaming of chasing a donkey, stumbling on a twisted olive tree branch, losing his balance and falling into a dark void. Suddenly, he is in a room, where he sits with four other men. The deep, watery gurgle of a nargila fills the space, sending grey clouds up to the ceiling and back down. Serpentine Arabic music twists into his dream and a belly dancer appears from behind a thick bluish haze. She moves her hips to the durbakki beat, making her way seductively towards him. A dancing shadow like the petals of a flower softly trembling in the naseem of an uncalm spring. The music stops abruptly and Maisoon's voice comes through the misty spaces between dream and reality. He sits up in bed, recognizing the music of the dream as the ringtone of her mobile. She's in the kitchen, talking in a hushed voice.

Quarter to six, Saturday morning. Again. They planned to take the camera and drive to the Carmel mountains to capture the changing leaves and budding flowers. Spring was only a fleeting moment in Haifa, soon to turn to suffocating heat. Now the buds will remain un-imprisoned, the leaves will turn brown and then dissolve into the ground uncaptured. He knows this even before Maisoon walks back into the bedroom to announce her important news. Change of plans. Instead of the Carmel mountains, the gas tank will be wasted on a highway. An hour-and-a-half ride in each direction. To pick up two people—father and son.

"We have to hurry, they only have a five-hour permit. I'll tell you everything on the way." Except about that all-too-familiar click at the end of the conversation. And the static preceding it, she thinks as she makes a pot of coffee for the road while he shaves. She knows that the mukhabarat target activists, monitor their emails and phone calls, but she had never thought she was important enough for them to notice her.

Ziyad stares at his reflection, his dark brown eyes narrowing. Father and son. A permit for five hours. Which checkpoint this time? He tilts his head back as he scrapes the blade close to his Adam's apple. He tries to calculate how much gas will remain in the car when the day tucks itself into the horizon. This will be the first time he has ever accompanied her.

Half an hour later they are on the highway that snakes its way south of Haifa, Maisoon putting the pieces of the story together. An eleven-year-old daughter. Motherless. Fragments of a missile intended for someone else shattering her body in half. Splintering a whole family in one breath.

Ziyad's face is a rock, eyes narrowly zeroed in on the road, not betraying a fraction of his emotions. Like any number of Saturdays, Tamar has taken their plans for the day, crumpled them up into a ball and thrown them in the dirt.

When they stop for gas, he studies her through the window; he is wondering if she feels guilty for dragging him into this but then he notices something. Her only mark of identity is the kohl on her eyes, which she painted on with a thin wooden brush. He has tried to decipher the kohl ritual for months. Most days she didn't bother with the glass bottle of night liquid. But then, some days it seemed to him she remembered owning it. Today he finally understands: she only wears it on days when she meets history. Days when she knows she is going to meet tradition. This is her way of belonging—of proving her own identity—to herself. Or to them?

Back on the road Maisoon continues telling him how they have ended up on the highway this Saturday instead of spending it hiking through the Carmel. She doesn't have all the details, but she is the only one whose phone was not off this Saturday morning. Eight months ago, Dunya, Abu Sufian's eleven-year-old daughter was on her way to a friend's house for a birthday party. A smothered drop of happiness in the midst of desolation. Her young body was caught by flying shards of a missile fired to assassinate somebody important—called an abominable terrorist by some, a fierce, courageous freedom-fighter by others. Maisoon doesn't know how she ended up in an Israeli hospital—not many are that lucky. Dunya's back was shattered and she was paralyzed from the neck down. Her father Abu Sufian and younger brother were allowed to stay with her at the hospital. Not much was left of her mother's body after the blast.

Yesterday, Abu Sufian received his first five-hour permit from the state security forces to leave the hospital—for the first time after months of crushing isolation. It is important that they be there for him, as there's no way of telling when he'll get another permit to leave the hospital smells behind—even for a few hours. The little boy is showing signs of distress.

At the entrance to the hospital, she stops to buy three cups of coffee and one hot chocolate. On Saturdays, the whole country comes to a halt. For God doesn't allow certain things on certain days. And so the elevator is on automatic, stopping on each floor for a whole minute before continuing on to the next. They climb the stairs to the fourth floor in slow motion, Ziyad trailing a few steps behind Maisoon, focusing on the paper tray of coffee and hot chocolate he's carrying. First floor—he realizes for the first time that Maisoon has two styles of clothes. For occasions such as these, her shirts tend to be a bit looser, hiding the gentle curves of her upper body. She is also less colourful, wearing solids of sadness. Second floor—he's thinking of Dunya, playing around with the sound of her name in his mind. Dunya—meaning world. He wonders why her parents gave her such a heavy name to drag with her for the rest of her life. Third floor—he's thinking of the five hours ahead of them. Did Maisoon mention anything about

Abu Sufian's life? He can't remember. By the time they reach the fourth floor, his armpits are damp and his shoulders tense.

Reaching the room at the end of the corridor, Ziyad suddenly realizes this is the first time he will meet a Palestinian from Gaza. He wants to turn around and leave. But he can't—he's carrying the coffee and hot chocolate. Five hours!

Maisoon falters at the half-open door, not wanting to interrupt the fragile intimacy within. Abu Sufian is combing his daughter's hair with delicate devotion, his back to the door. "Assalamu Alaikum," Maisoon says before entering the room. The face that turns to look at her has eternal grief engraved into the dark creases of the forehead.

In the far corner of the room, under the window, a rolled-up mattress and two bulging bags of sturdy black nylon. Maisoon quickly gathers her erupting emotions and tucks them away. Glancing at Ziyad, she motions with her head towards the little boy sitting on the bare floor with a sheet of paper and a single blue pastel, drawing a blue sky, blue tree, blue sun and blue grass. She quickly produces a small box of pastels from her backpack and hands them to Ziyad, "Here, make yourself useful."

She then walks over to Dunya and Abu Sufian—in fake confidence. "Marhaba habibti," she smiles at the paralyzed girl, sitting down on the corner of the bed. "I'm Maisoon, and that's Ziyad. We came from Haifa this morning."

"Is he your husband or brother?" Dunya is looking with curiosity at Ziyad.

"He's ... a good friend. I don't have a car, and it's Saturday, so he drove me here." Maisoon follows Dunya's eyes, which have now moved to the hot chocolate in her brother's hand. "Hey," Maisoon lowers her voice to a whisper now, "I got the hot chocolate for your brother because I didn't want him to feel left out that I didn't get him anything. I got you something very special."

"A book?" Dunya's eyes widen. The cover has one word: Joni. Under the title, a young woman in a wheelchair, her face turned to the camera

92

with a smile, holding a pen between her teeth. A stand propped up in front of her with a horse half drawn.

"Joni is a special girl. I think you will like the book."

"But I can't ..."

Before she can finish her sentence, Maisoon is busy arranging a stand on the table at the side of the bed, opening the book to the first page.

"Now, there you go," she winks at Dunya. "When you're done reading the first two pages, you just ask your brother or baba to turn the page."

When the young Jewish nurse walks in half an hour later, little Sufian is proudly taping his new masterpiece on the wall. Blue sky, a tree with a brown trunk and green leaves, red and orange flowers, and a scorching yellow sun. Ziyad and Abu Sufian sit in one corner of the room, heatedly discussing something. Maisoon is painting Dunya's nails in bright red. Abu Sufian gets up to greet the nurse in his heavily accented Hebrew. He talks to her for a few minutes, and then goes to Dunya's bedside.

"Dunya habibti, we will be back soon. I love you more than the moon," he kisses her forehead.

ديفا فراجمنتس

Abu Sufian received his five-hour permit into his cracked hands yesterday, minutes before touching his forehead in passion to the handwoven rug arranged on the stone cold sterile hospital tiles for his worship. With flames of devotion sizzling up on his insides, afraid he would miss a beat—a syllable, he had folded up the permit in a perfect half, tucking it into his shirt pocket. Only its edge peeked out at the white corridors, reminding him that he was a guest here. An unwanted visitor. Stating to the world with loud black letters, commas and dots that he needed a special permit to leave the hospital. What if. What if he were to walk out the glass doors with his son and cross to the other side of the street—of the world—to the park? Would anybody notice?

They are sitting on a cracked-up bench at the edge of the park now, Abu Sufian's eyes follow his little boy running from the swing to the slide and back to the swing. The sadness that he so carefully guards for the sake of his children is now draining out. "I don't understand these Yahud. With one hand they kill us, and with the other hand they offer us life. I really don't understand them."

This is not the first time Maisoon has heard this exact same sentence, spoken in various circumstances by those hurt and saved simultaneously by the same people. She understands perfectly well why they engage in these acts of grace. But she can't give voice to her anger—not to Abu Sufian, not to little Ahmad, not to any of them.

Abu Sufian was outside of the refugee camp on the day of the assassination. Retelling the story, his every word is pregnant with guilt. Because he wasn't there to save his wife. Because he was out looking for work. Because his car radio broke down and so he couldn't listen to the news. Because Dunya will never attend another birthday party in her shattered life. One thousand times because. He has reconstructed the events of that day from the fragmented scraps of Dunya's damaged memory and from what little Sufian could add to it.

On her way to the birthday party, Dunya had picked up a piece of paper dropped an hour before by an airplane. The paper told her to immediately evacuate the neighbourhood. She clutched it to her fluttering chest and hurried along the dirt road, stepping between puddles of countless other pieces of paper with the same horrifying one-line message. Her mother, who came out of the house just moments after Dunya left to hang laundry in the yard, saw the scattered papers on the ground. Must have thought kids were playing. Until she realized there were thousands of them. And then she would have heard it. The silence at the bottom of the ocean. In the middle of the earth. She picked up one piece of paper—in slow motion. Then, in demented madness she started running. For Dunya. Her world. Her laughter. Dunya looked back to see her mother's hair flying with the wind—thought about its unveiled beauty—and smiled at her. The last thing her eye caught before the explosion was the sheer terror in her mother's eyes. The last word she heard was the scream that was her name.

حيفا فراجمنتس

"Just drop me off at the entrance to the Wadi," Maisoon says in a flat voice as they enter Haifa.

"I thought we would ..." Ziyad glances at her.

"No habibi, I've got some work I need to get done, and then I want to catch up on some sleep. But next weekend maybe we can do something," she pauses. "Just the two of us, maybe hiking or something."

"Yeah, whatever. I'm sure Tamar will take care of that. What, no sick kids next Saturday? No checkpoints? Or maybe Abu Sufian will get another permit and we can spend the whole day with him and little Sufian again. How about it, huh?" Ziyad can't contain his anger any more.

"I can't believe you're actually saying this, Ziyad! After you've seen Dunya, how can you? You know what, just drop me off right here. Just stop the car!" Maisoon is almost screaming at him.

Ziyad stops the car, some three kilometers from Wadi Nisnas, and she opens the door and jumps out. Knowing Maisoon and her mad outbursts, he shouldn't be surprised, but he is. "Oh, you and your values," he says to the darkness of the car. He watches her walk for a few minutes, sure she'll come back. But she doesn't. You're so stubborn, Mais. I should just leave you and find myself a good woman to marry and have kids with. Who needs your politics and your Palestinians anyway? Getting back on the road, he heads to the German Colony to one of the cafés.

Maisoon doesn't mind the walk. Her body is stiff from the drive and hyped from all the coffee she's had today. The evening air is not stifling for a change, and a cool naseem blows from the direction of the Carmel mountain.

95

When she gets home, she automatically turns on the computer and puts on water for na'ana shai. The news on her Internet homepage features a short item:

> **IDF killed a fourteen-year-old Palestinian girl on her way to school.** Military sources regret the incident, admitting it was a mistake. The girl walked into a 'sterile area' and the soldiers suspected the schoolbag she was carrying contained explosives. The case is being investigated by the IDF.

She quickly surfs away from the page—unable to contain any more for the day. Puts Fairouz on YouTube and opens her sketchbook. She spends several hours carefully studying the composition of each piece, writing down notes. They are mostly pieces she knows will never sell—too 'exotic' for Amalia's taste. But she loves them anyway, and savours the time she spends on their two-dimensional shapes, perfecting each piece meticulously. One day, you will become real and I will feel your texture between my fingers.

حيفا فراجمنتس

After the hospital visit, Maisoon distanced herself from Ziyad. When he called, she was often too busy to talk to him for more than a few minutes. Her life was moving on. She was spending four days a week at the boutique and Amalia was including her in the management side of the business as well. The rest of the week she was busy working on new designs. On some Friday nights, Tayseer picked her up for a raw session of music; those nights were what kept her sane, letting the music flow through her, unwinding her body through dance.

Shahd now occupied Ziyad's corner of the diwan. Her dream of studying medicine was shelved for the time being; she had to wait her turn. Salam, her older brother was on a full scholarship in Italy, studying business management and working as a bartender to help his family. He'd promised his little sister that if she couldn't get a scholarship, he'd help her as much as he could. But she needed to have saber and wait— maybe another year or two. Meanwhile, she was working at Dar El Amal, helping Qais several days a week. For lack of any medical training, she was in charge of almost everything other than the health clinic. Her meagre salary made it possible to help out her family and to make the trip to Haifa almost every weekend. Still, she wasn't able to put any money aside for her studies.

It was Friday night; Maisoon and Shahd were enjoying the naseem coming in from the sea, scattering the odours of the souk in the Wad. Shahd had appeared on Maisoon's doorstep the night before, her arms scratched and her boots caked with mud. Maisoon had known not to ask any questions. As Maisoon didn't have to be at the boutique on Fridays they had spent the day at Al-Quds getting a lift with Tayseer in his old car. He was spending the weekend in East Al-Quds with some rapper friends and told Maisoon they could take the car back to Haifa, since there were no buses on Friday evening. He'd take the bus back on Sunday.

It was Shahd's first time in Al-Quds and she was as excited as a little girl. She greeted women doing their shopping with a smile, stopped to smell the oranges at one stall, tasted the roasted peanuts at another. Maisoon could barely keep up with her. But what each of them carried back to Haifa was as different as the vast distance between their separate worlds. Maisoon never failed to bring back the remains of the electricity she felt every time she visited the old city. For Shahd, her first time was overpowering, with a conflation of the kaleidoscopic images encapsulated in an unnaturally concentrated dose.

It's close to midnight, Al-Quds now but a memory, as they sit on the balkon. Maisoon is watching Um Tawfiq's laundry fluttering in the breeze, faintly aware of Shahd's playful hands massaging the back of her neck. She closes her eyes and thinks of Ziyad's hands. Wine is spreading in a warm trickle inside her body.

97

"You are so tense, Maisoon. Try to relax your body a little." Shahd's voice is a whisper.

Maisoon closes her eyes and thinks about Shahd's desire to become a pediatrician. She remembers their first meeting at the henna, the accidental brush of the hand, once, twice. She focuses her mind on this young woman, not so different from her. They both have dreams and they are both pursuing them in ways that are permitted to them. But where Maisoon is moving forward, Shahd's life seems to be stagnating. Put on pause by the Occupation. "Shahd, I'm trying to think how we can speed up this medical school thing. You can't just wait for Salam or a scholarship. We need to be active here. Do something."

Shahd's hands drop from Maisoon's shoulders. "How exactly is that possible in my part of the world? I'm doing the best I can. What else should I do?" As quickly as Shahd's anger rose, it subsides, "Just forget it. Your whole body is just one big tensed-up muscle. Come and lie down on the diwan, I'll give you a nice long massage. You got some olive oil?"

Maisoon, tired and dizzy from the wine, takes off her gallabiyya and lies face-down on the diwan. Shahd crouches down beside her, massaging her neck and shoulders, moving slowly down to Maisoon's back. Maisoon struggles hard not to think of Ziyad but her body isn't complying. She is slipping away into a half dream state—Ziyad is caressing her while Shahd continues to massage her back. Time waking and time dreaming are all blurred by the wine, hands are moving up and down her back shoulders neck calves thighs. She falls away and comes back—the hands now stroking her hair.

"Tell me a story, Shahd," she whispers.

Shahd's soft voice comes in gentle, soothing waves. "I will tell you the history of the sadness as glimpsed in Um Loai's eyes every time somebody calls out her name. She was Um Loai, and would remain Um Loai, even though Loai is no longer. Remember that day you asked my mama when are you going to finally meet this Loai? I saw her shrinking back in grief, then composing herself again and giving you a sad smile, offering more kahwa."

98

Shahd fiddles with a strand of Maisoon's hair. "I walked around with grief and sadness inside me. So heavy in there. And when I almost gave in, it started raining. I grabbed Loai's heavy coat, put the hood over my head, and took my pain, sadness and grief for a walk in the rain. Without an umbrella. I felt so close to him. Loai loved the rain. I hate it. I let the rain soak my body to the bone. I walked in the rain, smiling. Touching the drops of rain, catching them through the air before they dropped dead on the ground. Then ... laughter. I couldn't stop, laughter the next level of grief.

"He was shot dead at a demonstration. The only demonstration he ever went to, Mais. My brother never cared for the struggle really. Loai just wanted to get out of here. He didn't care about studies, but he made sure he was the first in his class just so he could get a scholarship abroad and leave this desolate place. And he got the scholarship. But then, just a few weeks before he was supposed to leave for England, he decided that he had to go to this demonstration. Just so he could say that he had done something for the struggle. Anything, really. It's not like he put too much thought or effort into it. There was a demonstration, it was close to home, and convenient for him. Nobody thought it would get violent. But it did. And Loai never made it home alive. Yes, of course there was an investigation, but no one was brought to trial. The soldier who shot him is probably just finishing his university studies, thinking of marrying his girlfriend, and planning their honeymoon somewhere in Europe. Maybe Paris ... or Rome. And Loai never even left the mukhayyam ... he never had the chance to brag to his fellow English students that he'd been to a demonstration ...

"You have your nice little apartment here, Mais, and you've got your education, and you're financially independent. You don't lack anything. You have a brother who's not thinking of blowing himself up and parents you can fall back on. Ah, tayyeb, so your life's constantly interrupted because you're a Palestinian. Like when you feel you don't belong or aren't wanted. But with us, it's the complete opposite—rare moments of happiness are what actually interrupt our lives."

99

Maisoon rolls onto her side, Shahd is crying and hugging herself. "Hey, hey, come over here," Maisoon pulls Shahd to her. She runs her fingers down Shahd's hair, then her back.

They stay like this for a long time with Shahd's head cradled against Maisoon's neck. Slowly, Maisoon becomes aware of Shahd's breath. At first it has the pull of grief but soon it changes and comes with weight and a quiver. Maisoon is soon only aware of her neck and Shahd's breath and when she feels lips pause at her neck, she groans. They lift their heads and look at each other as if asking permission. Their kiss is tender and long, each tasting the other one's sorrow. After that, they lie down, hugging, Shahd moves her hand up and down Maisoon's back, while Maisoon's hand softly plays with Shahd's hair. Shahd is about to say something, but Maisoon silences her.

"Hush, no need to say anything. Now go to sleep. I love you."

# 15

Maisoon woke up in a daze to clatter coming from the kitchen. The memory of Loai was lodged in her mind. *Did I dream him?* But then there was more—slowly all of it came back to her. She rolled over and buried her face in the pillow. A waft of kahwa mingled with the smell of a shakshooka reached her and she felt a sudden pang of hunger. A giggle and a snort. Shahd was talking with someone, her sentences interrupted by bursts of laughter.

"Oh you should see her when she's working. Not even a katyusha could make her get up from her worktable!"

*Ziyad! What's he doing here?* She threw the blanket off, discovered she was wearing only underwear, grabbed a scarf, wrapped it around her upper body, looked at the clock, blinked. *One o'clock.* She walked into the kitchen.

"Well, good morning, beauty!" Ziyad was sitting at the table, a cup of kahwa sada in front of him; Shahd was stirring the shakshooka on the stove.

Maisoon stood in her kitchen, her mind paralyzed. *I need to talk to Shahd.* But there was nothing she could do about it now. She managed to give Shahd a faded, embarrassed smile, then walked towards Ziyad, hugged him and sat on his lap.

"I missed you, hayati," he whispered in her ear, then louder, for Shahd to hear, in a playful tone, "ever since this Falasteeniyya came, you've forgotten all about me."

Shahd giggled and winked at Maisoon.

"We'll talk later," was all Maisoon could mumble in Shahd's direction.

They ate, making enough noise for a big family. When Shahd got up to wash the dishes, Ziyad stopped her, telling her that in this apartment, dishes had enough decency to patiently wait for two, sometimes three days in the sink. Maisoon searched Shahd's face for some traces of last night, but her eyes were playful, as they often were, and she couldn't tell what was hidden behind them.

In the afternoon, Shahd and Ziyad—like two conspirators—decided to clean the apartment and sent Maisoon to do some 'fresh' sketches on the balkon, because she was getting 'in their way'. She watched them from her comfortable exile; Ziyad clumsily tried to keep up with springy Shahd. They looked as if they'd been friends for ages. She wondered how come they were suddenly so close. Ziyad, who didn't want to have anything to do with any Palestinians. Shahd, who couldn't comprehend that Ziyad didn't feel he was a Palestinian. Shahd, who wanted to become a daktora so that she could give a piece of herself to the children of Palestine. Ziyad, who couldn't care less about the suffering of those living beyond his world. Did something happen between them while she slept? They were talking about me ...

"Hey Mais, where's the vinegar?" Shahd shouted from the kitchen.

"Top cabinet, left. Why would you need ..." But before completing her sentence, she remembered Um Loai explaining to her how vinegar was the best cleaning material for just about anything.

When they were done, Ziyad left for his place to take a shower and come back later; they planned to go down to the beach that night. Shahd came out of the shower wrapped up in a white robe and dropped onto the diwan. Maisoon put down Ahdaf Soueif's *In the Eye of the Sun* and kicked back, glad to be finally alone with Shahd.

"Shahd?" She wasn't sure how to approach the subject.

"Yes?" Shahd's eyes were sparkling.

102

"Listen, about last night ... what happened between us ... uh ... you know ..." she felt her face blushing. Shahd looked as if she were enjoying Maisoon's struggle.

"Oh, Maisoon," she scuttled closer to Maisoon and reached for her hand, gently caressing it. "I know you're with Ziyad and I know you love him. But I also know that I love you. You're my best friend. Do I want to make love to you? I won't deny it." She paused and looked Maisoon in the eyes to let her words sink in.

Maisoon felt Shahd was closing in on her.

Shahd, sensing Maisoon's rising panic, quickly continued, "I don't know if that makes me a lesbian, I'm also very attracted to men. But I fell in love with you when I saw you dancing that first night we met." She let go of Maisoon's hand and shifted back a little. "I don't understand why love has to be so complicated. I want to love you, and I want to fall in love with a man."

Maisoon shifted uncomfortably on the diwan, trying to understand what Shahd was saying. She was confused, it's not how she had planned this conversation. She was the one who was supposed to be in charge. "Look, Shahd, you know I love you too, and I wanted that intimacy with you last night as much as you did. I didn't think about it ... it just happened. But today ..."

"I know. You're worried about our friendship."

"Yes ... I mean no. We've become so close. I do love you, and I don't want to lose you as a friend. And then there's Ziyad ..."

Shahd reached again for Maisoon's hand, "Mais, habibti, I'm not saying we should become a couple! Don't worry, I won't take you from Ziyad. And I'm not expecting anything from you. I just don't want things to change between us because of last night. What happened happened. I think we can leave it at that." She got up from the diwan, "Agreed?"

Maisoon was dazed. Slowly, she got up from the diwan and embraced Shahd in a big hug. "Agreed."

In the evening, while they ate sandwiches on the diwan, Maisoon remembered Shahd's plans. "You know, what we talked about last night

... your medical school ... well, I have an idea." She smiled and told Shahd that she could teach her how to work with silver—to begin with, she would show her how to wrap the silver around the stones, hammer, do the connecting rings that held the different pieces together. She'd then show her how to set the stones securely in place. Business was good; Amalia was selling one of her lines to a boutique in Jaffa, and was attracting some interest from international markets. "I can't keep up with it on my own. I need help, and you need money."

"But Mais, I don't know anything about jewellery design. And I don't have the time. Remember my work at Dar El-Amal?"

"I have it all figured out. Just listen to me and think about it. You don't have to quit your job, I would never ask you to do that. But you're here almost every weekend anyway. So, instead of just drinking wine and going to the beach and messing with my man, you can spend several hours working with me. We'll do it together, don't worry. And if it doesn't work out, then you'll know that at least you tried."

Not convinced, Shahd noncommittally promised she'd think about it.

ديفا فراجمنتس

The night was all sticky when they walked through the souk and they were glad to reach the seashore, where the wind was tasting salty along with carrying grains of sand that stuck to their bodies. Ziyad and Shahd were walking ahead of Maisoon, talking. Maisoon was dragging herself behind them, still wondering about Ziyad's sudden reappearance after weeks of silence. And Shahd and what it all meant.

Shahd had her kafiyyah wrapped loosely around her shoulders; she didn't have to think twice before putting it on. Maisoon felt a pang of jealousy at Shahd's easy expression of her identity. It was a natural extension of her. And then there was her boisterous laughter—flung in all directions. When they were out, she was always loud, drawing on the ends of her words, marking them with punctuation marks, adding invisible—but visibly heard—exclamation marks. She would start singing Fairouz without warning just at a moment when a group of young soldiers would be passing by, fearless to assert her roots and original ownership of this land stolen from under her grandparents' feet.

Maisoon thought of her own identity. No, she didn't feel wholly Falasteeniyya. She vehemently refused the adjective 'Israeli' that was forced on her. She was a woman with freedoms that Shahd simultaneously admired and abhorred. But still she felt trapped. Between her father's haunting past and her own tomorrows. And now this confusion with Shahd. She'd never considered being with a woman before, but with Shahd, it seemed so natural, so ... She caught up with Ziyad and Shahd, they stepped to the side to let her in between them. Shahd smiled at her, and Maisoon saw desire in her eyes. Oh what have you done to me, Shahd?

They reached Tal E-Samak, the hill which always seemed so out of place right there at the beach. On the top, a young man, alone with his durbakki, was sitting on a rock, his back to the three approaching shadows.

"Hey, Tayseer! We brought you the birthday girl," Ziyad grinned. Shahd tied a scarf around Maisoon's waist, Tayseer drummed softly.

"Happy birthday Mais!"

Her birthday had completely slipped out of her mind. Twenty-eight years. A bottle of red wine was opened. A woman, a brother, a lover and a friend got drunk, danced ... laughed ... and then watched the sky turn from black to grey to dark blue.

# 16

ذ The following week, Maisoon remains in her apartment, working on several new designs incorporating the coins Um Loai has given her. When Amalia sees some of the sketches, she suggests Maisoon email them to Adon Yuval, a Jewish jewellery trader from Amsterdam who visited her boutique recently and asked about jewellery with a local touch. He is looking to expand his business and was searching for something fresh and new.

The short response comes a few days later:

"Thank you. I would like to see some samples of these before we proceed. Can you ship some by express mail as soon as possible?"

Maisoon is thrilled, she's been given a chance to prove her talent and stay true to herself. But it proves more challenging than she thought it would be. All the techniques she knows are failing her. It is Shahd who finally sees the flaw one evening when Maisoon is close to giving up.

"It's not working, Shahd. I'll never be able to make a whole collection out of these. I'm not even sure of what I'm doing." She is close to tears.

Shahd looks at the rough cupronickel coins and the small blue eyes on the side of the table, then at the tools to the left. Finally, she looks at Maisoon triumphantly. "Mais! Forget all of this," pointing to the open book on the most recent techniques. "You're trying to apply new techniques to something ancient. It's not about technique! Think. Why are you using authentic coins? You want to bring history and our existence into your designs. That takes much more than technique."

"Uh ... what are you trying to say?" Maisoon gets up from the diwan and walks over to the worktable to stand by Shahd.

"Can't you see it, Mais? These techniques—they're just not intended to make this kind of jewellery."

Maisoon studies the book, as if seeing it for the first time. Then she moves her gaze to the right, picks up one glass blue eye, moving it close to her face, feeling its rough texture between her fingers. She holds it up to the light—translucent, its dark blue turned into sea blue. Holding it against the table and close to it, it becomes dark grey. Changing like the desert, yet remaining the same. Constancy. Then the coins. Pieces of real history. We're not an invented people. "I think you're right, Shahd. Almost. It's not just that, there's something else to it which I still lack."

"And that would be ...?"

"Courage to cross the line. Between art for the sake of art and beauty, and art as a tool for political expression." She puts the cupronickel coin back on the table in resignation. "I don't think I have this ability in me, Shahd."

She turns her back on the table and her friend and walks out to the balkon for a cigarette. Shahd lets Maisoon have her moment of despair.

A soft knock from the inside before the door opens and Shahd walks onto the balkon with a warm blanket, a tray with two glasses of shai and a trail of steam. Maisoon smiles despite the tears. Shahd moves the sabra to the edge of the coffee table, sets the tray next to it and sits down opposite Maisoon so that she can see her face. "So?"

"So what, Shahd?" her voice is jumpy.

"Well, I was thinking about your proposal to work with you, since I see now that you could use some help." She is hiding her smile behind her glass of tea, but Maisoon can hear it in her voice.

The wicker chair creaks as Maisoon straightens up, but almost immediately she slumps back, pulling her legs up and closing in on herself. "It won't work, Shahd. It just won't. I tried so hard. I'm a failure."

"Wait a minute, don't move!" Shahd jumps up from her chair and runs back to the diwan. She comes back with Maisoon's sketchbook. She opens it up on the sketches Maisoon did with the coins. "Look, it's all in here. How can you even say that you're a failure! These sketches, when you make them into jewellery, will take Amalia's breath away, not to speak of your Yahudi trader in Amsterdam! They're out of this world."

Maisoon feels anger rising at Shahd. "You don't know anything about it, Shahd. Do you have any idea how hard this will be? I should never have thought I could do it!" She stretches her legs, making to get up.

Shahd pushes her back into the chair. "No!" Her voice is rising and echoing through the souk. The purple in her eyes is becoming darker.

"How dare you!" Maisoon grabs her glass of shai and smashes it against the tiles. She tries to grab her sketchbook, but Shahd, sensing danger, shoves it behind her back and falls back into a chair pressing into it. Maisoon lunges at Shahd's back and screams. Losing her balance, she almost falls on top of Shahd.

"Wha ... Mais?"

Maisoon slumps back into her chair in pain, holding her right foot up in the air. Little drops of dark red blood decorate the tile right below her foot. Both women stare at the blood, Maisoon in pain, Shahd in confusion.

"You just had to break that glass!"

"Everything all right there, sabaya?" It was Um Tawfiq's voice coming from across the alley. She was peeking from behind the laundry, more out of curiosity than concern.

"Salam, Um Tawfiq. We're fine, I just stepped on a piece of glass, but it's all right, really."

The older lady stands like a sentinel for a few minutes before withdrawing in disappointment. Maisoon and Shahd watch the balkon door swing shut behind her. They look at each other, then down at the blood.

Maisoon bursts into laughter. "Now see what you made me do!"

Shahd joins in the laughter and plants a kiss on Maisoon's forehead.

Shahd stays in Haifa for two weeks working with Maisoon. At first, she does the simple tasks, making sure they always have hot shai with fresh na'ana, setting up the table, running downtown to get more supplies. Then she is studying the sketches, commenting, helping to choose the right colours of stones, and the sizes of the blue eyes and cupronickel coins.

حيفا فراجمنتس

Maisoon walks into Amalia's boutique, sleepless nights weighing down her eyes. She takes a small black velvet pouch from her bag and hands it to Amalia. A turquoise necklace of a design Amalia has never seen before, small coins dangling from thin strips of varying length, shining in the light coming through the blinds in stripes. "It's our new line, all the way to Amsterdam."

Amalia purses her lips while she studies this unexpected design. She fingers one of the cupronickel coins, then notices it has writing on it. On one side it says Palestine in Arabic, Hebrew and English, with the year 1927, and on the other it reads 10 mils.

Maisoon knows she is taking a big chance. "They're authentic," she almost whispers. It was one of the coins Um Loai had given her.

"I can see that much." Maisoon can hear the hesitation in Amalia's voice. "I also see that you're beginning to discover your own style. And that you're trying to make a political statement with your art." There was a hint of disapproval.

"I know it's not the soundest business choice, Amalia, but I have to remain true to myself."

"Not sure it's a good choice for Adon Yuval, but it's your decision, and I'm sure you've weighed your options well."

The day before the meeting with Adon Yuval, Amalia calls, "There's a slight change in plans."

Maisoon hesitates, expecting bad news.

"He wants to come and see the new line at your studio."

Studio? What studio? Maisoon looks around at her diwan. "I see, Amalia. Is there any chance that ..."

"No, he insists. I knew you wouldn't like it, so I tried to persuade him to meet you at the boutique but it was like talking to a wall. I'm sorry."

"He wants to come here," she tells Shahd as she puts down the phone. "I'm not sure I want him in here. I mean, this is my home. I don't just let anyone come in here."

Sitting at the worktable, Shahd looks around, seeing the simple sacredness of this place for the first time. In one corner stands an empty bottle of wine, red ringed stains surround it, incrimination of many more bottles. Next to the bottle, the small wooden box containing the stuff of hallucination. On the old yellow coffee table, some of Majid's writings. On the diwan, a fraying blanket. And the shawls scattered about. She now understands the rush in her blood every time she runs up the stairs. This place is also a sanctuary for her. Allowing her the space she's never had in her life. Suddenly she understands Maisoon's obsession with privacy and why Maisoon feels so protective of this space. It gives her freedom. But she also knows that Maisoon's mark on this place will not be rubbed away by a stranger's visit.

حيفا فراجمنتس

It was also the first time Amalia had visited Maisoon. Shahd opened the door for them—first Adon Yuval walked in, followed by Amalia. Immediately they felt his awkwardness upon realising how overdressed he was. This was not the kind of business meeting he was used to. Until now, he'd never worked with any unknown—let alone local—artists. He scanned the room in distaste, finally identifying it as Maisoon's studio—among other things.

"So ... this is where you made that exquisite necklace," he motioned with his head towards the worktable, again, with that same expression of distaste.

110

"Would you like to see the pieces I've been working on?" Maisoon asked in agitation.

"Yes, of course. It's the main purpose of my visit here."

While Shahd went to prepare shai, Maisoon spread the new pieces on her worktable. The trader picked up the first piece—a ring—with extreme care, studied it for several minutes, and moved to the next one, a bracelet. He repeated this for all the items. When he was finished, he drank his steaming glass of shai, took out a pack of cigarettes and searched for an ashtray. When he finally saw one, he breathed out and lit a cigarette without asking if it was okay.

"It's not really what I had in mind, you know," he said between puffs of smoke. "We're not going to sign a contract."

Maisoon felt a nerve above her eye flicker.

"Not the regular kind, I mean." He tapped his cigarette over the ashtray. "We're going to work per order. I pay you 40 per cent in advance, and the balance on receipt of shipment. All prices should be calculated in euro. You will be given advanced notice of an order so I do not expect there to be any problem with you delivering it on time."

Maisoon exhaled and shivered at the same time but she forced herself to look at him with what she hoped was a look of confidence.

He finished his cigarette in silence and stood up. Taking an envelope from his breast pocket, he handed it to Maisoon. "The price I agreed on with Amalia. There's an address in there where to ship this order."

After they left, Maisoon looked at Shahd in disbelief. "I don't think he noticed the coins. As a matter of fact, I'm sure he didn't. Otherwise the deal would be off."

"Well, we are definitely not going to draw his attention to them!" Shahd said as she hugged her friend.

# 17

Asmahan                                                  أسمهان

When you go, you can't love me any more. Your love becomes a memory. You can't love someone you can't touch.

Come, let me hold you, let me put some hugs in a small cloth pouch, and whenever I long for your touch, I can take a small bit of Hug out of the pouch. Just like you take a bottle of olive oil from your family's olive grove, and every time you miss home, you spill a drop onto your tongue and taste Home.

 Turning the page over, Maisoon read four sad words:

آسف خيّبت أملك أسمهان

—I'm sorry, I let you down Asmahan. From the date written on the first page, Maisoon could tell he wrote this short piece during his imprisonment, which clearly marked his breaking point. When he left prison, he was someone else. A disassembled, dispirited man who had lost everything: his passion for writing, his zeal for life, his fire for justice, and his love Asmahan.

She reached for another piece, written on unlined paper. The writing here was small and crammed, making the reading slower.

at the end of this corridor—on the second floor
of this stone house
there is an opening
with an iron bolt

two doors—light blue,
like the colour of grass when you look at it from a certain angle right
after shatwet Nisan.
the doors, when closed—always locked in a kiss.
just like that—with no shame at all.

When father forces their kiss away in the morning—they groan, slowly
turning away, each one facing another part of this corridor. Sometimes
they get to be reunited after a short while, because mother doesn't
like the draught much, so after an hour or two she walks up the stairs
to the second floor and makes them into lovers again. When that
happens, there's no groaning from the doors. I think mother does oil
their hinges every so often. With olive oil—anything other would be an
offence to these old wooden friends of hers.

I remember the day mother decided to put bars on the small
windows on the upper part of the two lovers. The frame—almost
collapsed from all that metal fitting, but survived—to the amazement
of father, who refused to pay for the bars. "Nobody can squeeze
through these windows, Widad!" he hollered from the diwan on the
ground floor. But she was determined, and paid Abu Hasan from her
own money.

The next day, early in the morning, father got out of his bedroom
and walked down the corridor. He forced the nightlong kiss of the old
wrinkled lovers apart. A sharp wind blew in. He closed the doors again.
Silently, obediently, they went back to their kiss. But father wanted to
air the corridor, so he unlatched the windows and pushed them out.
They didn't fly open. Their glass rattled as they smashed into the new

metal bars. Abu Hasan put the bars on the wrong side of the windows. "Widaaaaad!" father hollered, the glass rattled again as he banged the windows shut.

The bars remained there. Father never forgave mother for her stupidity. It became the story told over and over to anybody who happened to walk past these doors. But mother would just smile, "We are all entitled to small stupidities sometimes."

The doors have their own history, and if you come closer, you can read it in their cracks. I remember—I think I was about sixteen—hiding behind them, out on the balkon in just my shorts and a short-sleeved t-shirt in the middle of the night, from father's anger after he discovered my secret notebook. He burnt it—of course! He waited until morning and went to the garden. He set fire to it and made me watch. I saw the words and every letter curling up in the flames. I stood there shaking. He thought I was shaking from fear. But I was concentrating on the escaping words: I was trying to catch them as they spiralled in the flames. Sumud resistance fight back stand up never kneel down this earth my earth this land Falasteen. Then, when all that was left was thin grey smoke coiling up towards the west, I followed it and saw that it was in the direction of the balkon. I ran inside and took the stairs three at a time to reach these doors. I pulled them open and they groaned like always—only with mother are they quiet and obedient—and I stepped out and caught the smoke in my lungs. I breathed fast to get it all inside because that was all that was left of my words. So you see Asmahan they are literally inside me even now. I swallowed them whole.

After the burning, I didn't speak to father for two months. I spent the afternoons on this balkon, behind these doors. Mother kept stuffing money in my pocket so that I could buy a new notebook but I always returned it to her. I thought she was doing it more out of pity than understanding the significance of writing for me. You see, my mother never learned to read, and father never told her what he read inside my notebook on that day. But I was wrong about mother. I mistook her love for pity.

114

Well, mother was a very smart woman. She had this small trunk in her bedroom where she kept some things. So one day, when she could no longer bear the silence, she pushed the trunk through the corridor to the balkon. She brought two old wooden chairs from the garden and put one on either side. Then she went down to the salu and from the cupboards she brought up a deep red, hand-stitched tablecloth. It was square, and the trunk was rectangular, so she spread it diagonally across the trunk. She did all this while I was at school and father at work.

When I came back from school, she was standing in the doorway, smiling, and I knew she was waiting for me with some secret. I kissed her on the cheek, smelling olive oil soap. She didn't say a word, but motioned me inside. When I closed the door behind me, she turned back and put her hand inside the deep pocket of her abaya. She took out a brand new notebook, very thick and with a leather cover. Asmahan— real leather! She held it out to me but I shrank back. I thought, where is father, is this one of his tricks but it couldn't be because this is mother and she loves me and she would never do any ugly thing to me. She was still holding the notebook in her hand, extended in front of me, silently. I could smell the leather and I wanted to grab it and run ... where to I don't know. I took the notebook, and then I kissed her hand and took her other hand and held them both in front of my face. I put them on my cheeks so she could feel the tears. "Yamma," I whispered but she put her hand on my mouth and whispered back, "Don't say thank you. This is yours and you do what you think is right. But don't be angry with father. It's not good for your health."

I was young enough still to let mother touch my face, but old enough for anger that made my stomach twist. I threw the notebook at her feet, and ran up the stairs, hollering, "I hate him." I ran to the balkon—the doors were open to let in fresh air and sunshine. When I saw the chairs and the makeshift table with the burning red cloth I knew immediately I should not have turned my back on mother like that. But it was done—her own son had hurt her. Her only son. I felt such shame because I knew she did it for me although I didn't know yet that all this was devised carefully to deceive father.

I sat down on a broken chair and stayed there. I knew mother was downstairs, probably still standing there with the notebook at her feet. But my pride wouldn't let me go down to ask for forgiveness. After a while she came up. She came with shai—lots of sugar just the way I love it and with fresh na'ana, which she had picked from the garden. She put one glass on my side of the trunk and one glass on the other side. We sat there, silently watching the garden and the street beyond. Maybe an hour we sat like that … I don't know how long. I thought father would come home soon and discover the leather notebook.

I was getting sleepy but I was also stubborn and curious to see what mother would do. She sat there, her hands in her lap, looking down into the garden, ignoring me. I was beginning to think she'd forgotten I was even there. But then she turned to me, put her hand on mine and said, "I bought this notebook from my own money, Majid. It belongs to you. You can throw it away if you want, or you can write in it." And she took it out of the pocket of her abaya again and put it on the red cloth. I didn't touch it. I was scared, Asmahan, to even hope that I would be able to write again and not see the words curling up in smoke. Mother saw the fear in my eyes, smiled, then reached for the cloth and uncovered the trunk partially to reveal the heavy lock on its side. She didn't have to say anything. When she saw my face widening in a smile, she closed her hand on mine, dropping into it a small key. Then she stood up and went downstairs to prepare dinner.

I stayed there on the balkon and soon it was dark. The notebook still lay on the trunk and the key was still in my palm. Then I heard the gate opening and closing, father was home from work. I quickly unlocked the trunk. It was full of small brass objects. I took some out and put the notebook in and then put the objects carefully on top and I locked the trunk and pulled the cloth over its edge so that it hid the lock. I went into my room and lay on my bed until I heard father's heavy footsteps walking tiredly up the stairs and into his bedroom. Then I waited some

116

more until I heard his faint snoring. I went downstairs to eat something and came back up to find the balkon doors slightly open. Mother knew I would come back for the notebook and she knew the doors would croak if I opened them. I sat on the broken chair for a long time, holding the notebook in both hands.

Then mother came up with a big round candle in a jar and she set it on the trunk, kissed me on the cheek and said good night ibni. The next thing I remember it was morning and I had filled twenty pages.

I went downstairs when I heard father leave for work. I ate, walked back upstairs like a ghost and dropped onto my bed. When I woke up, I looked through the window and saw the grey sky beginning to turn purple and red, finally settling on light blue; I'd slept the whole day and the whole night.

There's more, but suddenly Maisoon needs to see her father. She leaves the letter on the coffee table, grabs a sweater and hurries out the door.

"Baba, who was Asmahan?" Maisoon tries to sound casual. Majid is reading the newspaper, Maisoon stands with her back to him, facing the library. Running her fingers along the backs of the books, she stops at Ghada Karmi's *In Search of Fatima*. She takes the book off the shelf and faces her father.

Majid sighs. Folding the paper, he motions for Maisoon to sit. "So you're in search of Asmahan." He sits for a while gathering himself, reaching for his cigarettes, searching under the paper for the lighter. Then he leans back in his chair and looks beyond Maisoon, beyond the family home and into the past. "My friend Mahmoud had family relatives in Jenin and he invited me to come with him and spend Eid el Fiter there. I fell for Asmahan the moment I saw her. She had the most beautiful eyes in the world, deer's eyes, and the smile on her face just melted me. In the evening, Mahmoud and I put on a play for the family. Something we'd been working on together. Later she told me that she fell in love with my words first." Majid stops to let Maisoon take it in. Mahmoud, Eid el Fiter, Jenin. When he sees the sadness in her

117

eyes, he continues, "Yes, she was Muslim. After that first meeting, I visited her family as often as I could with Mahmoud who, seeing our love, would always come up with the right excuses. But as you know, our story didn't have a happy ending.

"Things went terribly wrong. She had two cousins who were involved in the armed resistance, and they manipulated me into collaborating with them. All I can tell you is that love is blind. All I breathed was Asmahan. Of course, her family didn't know about our love, they thought I was just Mahmoud's best friend. And Asmahan didn't know about her cousins' activities. Anyway, the mukhabarat were on my tail and it was just a matter of time. They followed my movements for months, and the next thing I knew I was thrown in jail. During that time, Asmahan lost all her zest for life, she lost weight and stayed in bed most days. Soon her family found out the cause. When I finally got out of jail, she was engaged to be married to an older cousin of hers. Her father thought it best, there were too many things against me, I wasn't a Muslim, I had a security-related history and I was from this part of the world.

"I think you've heard the story you came here for." Maisoon walks around the coffee table to her father and kneels in front of him. Majid's eyes are moist, "Mais? I wanted to tell you about ... you and Ziyad ..." She puts a finger on his lips, "You don't need to say it, Baba. I know." She kisses his cheek, "Thank you for telling me the story."

# 18

"Salam was on Skype with Mother last night ... he's getting married." Shahd announced dispassionately, the words wrapping around the thin paper she was cutting up into squares. They were sitting on the floor, packaging up the new pieces in small black pouches, ready to be shipped to Amsterdam.

Maisoon was busy writing down the details of the shipment in her log, while Shahd was packing each piece separately in delicate transparent paper before dropping them in their pouches. It was the second order in less than four months, and the tight deadline had crept up and stolen Maisoon's nights away.

Maisoon looked up from her log. "And? Isn't this what your mama has been waiting for?"

"Mais! He's marrying an Italian! Ajnabiyya, not one of our own." The thin square of paper ripped in two as Shahd pulled it too tight around a bracelet threaded with the tiniest of turquoise stones. "This is not exactly what my mother expected. They're doing this civil marriage thing ... Why are you smiling?"

"Ach, just thinking of what my mama told me that day when she came with me to your house. We are the same, after all. On both sides of the wall, we cling to tradition like a sweat-soaked shirt clings onto your back in the boiling sun of Tammuz. It's the glue holding us together as one people. Customs and traditions. It doesn't matter how much we've become modern, how much we've changed, or how much of our oppressive traditions we've shed on the way; there are things we just refuse to let go of." She paused, taken aback by this longing not to let go of tradition, when her most significant struggles in the past few years were all connected with freeing herself from its shackles.

"Customs and traditions ... so why can't Salam just understand this? And you know how things are done in these parts of the world ... As if there aren't enough nice girls around here. Even if she were ... like you ... from inside, but at least Falasteeniyya, not Ajnabiyya."

"Shahd ...? Are you listening to what you're saying? How can you say something so ... so ... absurd?"

Shahd ignored her, "Salam was always more Palestinian than me, at least in customs and traditions. He's always had a thing for tradition. And now ... now ... this!"

"I have a feeling you're the one finding it unbearable, not Um Loai. Am I right, Asal?"

Shahd looked up at Maisoon, her eyes reflecting bafflement. Her jaw muscles tensing, she opened her mouth to speak—to defend herself, but then the truth of Maisoon's words sunk in. "But how could he? I mean, how could he fall in love with someone who is so ... so ... so disconnected from ... this? Seriously, could you love Ziyad if he ... if he ... didn't walk the same earth as you do? If his blood didn't bubble the same way yours does at the sound of the durbakki? If your body didn't react the same way at the smell of nargila? Could you?"

"Shahd ... what is love anyway? I don't know if I love him. All I know is that when he touches me, I lose my balance. I lose my senses— my very self. Does it mean I love him? I don't know."

"You're avoiding my question, Maisoon."

"You know why. Because you're right. I never could. But it's just the way I am. Look, Asal ... I have this ... need ... for Ziyad to contain my pain. And he can only do it because he knows the same pain, inside and out."

Crossing her legs under her, Shahd stared at Maisoon uncomprehending. Love wasn't supposed to be this complicated. "I ... I meant something much simpler than that, Mais. I was just imagining a sister-in-law with whom I can talk about passing through checkpoints and she'd understand exactly what I was talking about. I just couldn't do that with an Ajnabiyya. It would just ... taste foreign."

"But we're talking about the same thing Shahd. The ability to really understand our experiences. No outsider can ever truly understand them. But people are different. Not everyone has this need from a partner. Take Qais, for example. He can easily fall in love with someone for her kind heart and pure soul."

Shahd straightened up at the mention of Qais, "How do you know that?"

"It's so obvious. It's in his eyes. Anyone can tell."

Shahd went quiet and returned to the packing. Maisoon watched Shahd and resisted an urge to push Qais and Ziyad aside and jump across the jewellery and kiss her. She was playing with fire.

She picked up her pen and went back to work. Half an hour later she stood up, "There we are. Now get dressed. You're coming with me to the post office to send this off."

ﺣﻴﻔﺎ ﻓﺮاﺟﻤﻨﺘﺲ

Two women walking down the stairs, hands full of promises, the light receding into darkness with each step. Um Muhammad is sweeping away the checkered squares of dust left by the spaces in the bottoms of the vegetable crates, now stacked—almost empty—one on top of the other.

Two women walking through the souk, arms heavy, wrapped around expectations. Abu Nidal is rinsing the copper finjans, stacking up the chairs, drinking his last finjan of kahwa with a loud sweeesh of the breath.

Two women—one from each side of the wall—taking the steps at the end of the Wad two at a time. In a hurry before the post office in

121

Hadar closes on their dreams. And they know that no matter the wall, permits, checkpoints or no-go areas—they are now walking together with a parcel of newly gift-wrapped hopes.

حيفا فراجمنتس

They retrace their steps back to the souk, taking the stairs that mark the boundary between Hadar and Wadi Nisnas—crossing lines invisible to Shahd but painful to Maisoon. There are parts of Haifa where the movement between neighbourhoods is like moving in and out of different worlds. Parts where she doesn't belong, others where she feels like a natural extension of the scenery. Other parts burst with a mixture of so many worlds that it seems impossible for them to be contained in a single street and yet they are.

Maisoon turns to Shahd, "So ... what about your plans, Asal? Medical school?"

Some boys are playing outside, chasing each other, their shrill voices rolling up the stone stairs, crossing the boundaries carelessly, unknowingly. Maisoon watches one of the boys as he disappears behind a stone wall. You still have time before you start drawing artificial lines.

Shahd crosses her arms as she walks, "I'd love to stay free like you, but it's not possible for me. I'm not built to make it on my own. Medical school?" Another boy bumps into Shahd, she shakes her head as he runs off hardly noticing her.

"I want to believe, Maisoon ... that whoever I marry will be supportive of my dream to be a daktora. But the decision will be his of course and I'll just have to adapt to it somehow. It's the ancient way, Mais. It's the way things are supposed to be done." Abu Nidal is gone now, leaving an empty space behind him. "Don't give me that look. I'm not like you. I'm not strong enough to stand up to tradition, and I'm not sure that I want to. Yes, I envy you, your freedom and independence, but don't tell me it comes without a price. I see how difficult it is for you sometimes. I don't want that in my life. I want to be comfortable, knowing there's someone stronger than me to fall back on. And if it means not going to medical school ..." her voice trails off.

That night Maisoon rolls a joint and they celebrate getting the shipment in on time. In the morning, Maisoon wakes up feeling the heaviness of Shahd's naked leg slung over her stomach. Maisoon remembers the heat of their passion and accepts it now as part of their friendship. She doesn't feel she is betraying Ziyad. Silently she slides out of bed, hoping Shahd will not remember what happened, yet knowing she will. She takes a quick shower before waking her up and sending an SMS to Ziyad. She needs to borrow his car so she can drive Shahd home.

## 19

Approaching the top of the hill that marks the edge of Tal E-Zeitun, Maisoon can see a long line of cars, slowly slithering towards the checkpoint. Small splashes of dark green are dashing between the cars—back doors and trunks are being flung open. Soldiers. Must be a warning. She glances at her watch. Ziyad will be furious. She can't remember if they made any plans for the evening. But even so, she is again driving his car. She reaches the line and stops behind a Mazda. It takes forty minutes to inch near the front, she counts eight cars in front of her, she looks in her rear vision mirror and sees a long line of cars behind. A big blotch of dark green walks slowly towards her. She holds her burning cigarette outside the window.

"Get out of the car."

Just out of high school, the blotch is giving her orders.

"Over there," he points his machine gun to a small group of people clustered at the wall of a low building to the left of the check-point.

She hesitates, looking around frantically for something familiar to hold on to. She feels a dull pain in her back, forcing her down on her knees. Dust rises into her face, she turns her head and looks up at the soldier blotch, he is smiling at her.

"Need help? Maybe another shove to make you move faster?"

She quickly scrambles up and hurries to join the others. Keep your head high. Don't let them see your humiliation. She watches as her car is being searched.

She looks around her. Two older women wearing veils, silently wait. They look like they've been through this many times before. A man in his sixties, chain-smoking, deep creases like dried-up tracks of a river on his forehead, is pacing the dirt road back and forth. Not with agitation, that wouldn't be safe to show here. He glances at the two veiled women every few minutes, mustering some words from under his white moustache. His voice is so low Maisoon can only make out the Inshallah inserted as if by magical force between every few words.

A small girl of four or five catches her eye. Black curls cover a delicate face, she's absorbed in drawing. Why does an angel like her have to go through this? Anger is rising in Maisoon's throat, but the girl's mother seems very much at ease. No panic in her eyes. No anger in her movements. Still they are suspects. Even them.

At the edge of the low building, four young men are leaning against the wall. All are smoking rolled cigarettes. Dark, handsome faces— unshaven. Ragged like their jeans. One of them keeps charging edgy glances at Maisoon. She can't read the emotion in his eyes—they are solid. Black. In an almost animal-like reaction, her body contracts.

When she looks away, she notices the foreigner. Yellow hair, faded with dust, partly concealing a pale face. She is sitting at the other end of the wall, her back against the raw unfinished building blocks. Though her eyes are darting from one soldier to the other, she seems quite at ease with the militant environment. This is incongruous with the image of most foreigners who seem to shrink at checkpoints; getting a wild trapped-animal look in their eyes. Maisoon watches her for a while with curiosity. The woman reaches into her backpack and takes out a sketchpad. She is drawing something, looking up every now and then at the soldiers. Maisoon walks the length of the wall towards her, her hand tracing the cracks between the blocks.

"Hey," she says as she sits next to her.

"Hey," the woman smiles at Maisoon and continues to draw.

"Can I see?" she indicates the sketchpad. The blonde woman nods. It is a rough sketch of the checkpoint—rugged soldier figures with machine guns, veiled women standing in a line. "They'll confiscate it, you know," Maisoon says.

"Let them. It's just practise. I've already got this place imprinted in my mind, and they can't confiscate that."

Maisoon smiles at the sauciness in the woman's voice. "Yeah, you're right. They've come a long way with all their technology, but they're still not that sophisticated."

"Are they going to arrest me? Will they put me in jail?" She asks while she focuses on the details of one of the soldiers' machine guns. "Do you think they'll call the embassy or let me at least call my parents?"

"It's my first time also ... I mean, being stopped like this ... I don't know ... but I'm sure it will be fine ... for you at least. We'll find out soon." The uncertainty in Maisoon's voice is soothing rather than alarming. For the next half hour, Maisoon listens to the last few days of this woman's discovery of hard-core Occupation.

"You! Come with me." The machine gun is pointing at Maisoon. She stands up to go, whispering a promise, "I'll wait for you at the other side."

She is led to a dingy room, with a metal table and two metal folding chairs. The room smells of stale tobacco, sweat, and something sour. The door closes behind her. Ten minutes later, the door opens and a man in civilian clothes walks in.

"You are aware that this is a closed zone to Israelis?"

I'm not an Israeli. He doesn't wait for her answer and begins pounding questions—where has she been, who has she met, who does she know. Her father had warned her of this. Just act stupid, answer the questions and whatever you do—don't lie! They have their ways of knowing everything. And don't volunteer any extra information.

"So, how often do you come here?"

Thin strips of sweat are streaming down her back. She concentrates on the question, figuring out if the times passed through the no-go area

126

count. "About once every three or four months," her voice is dry and scratchy.

"I see. And where do you spend your time?"

Maisoon's mind spins fast. Need something good ... Baba said not to lie ... but I can't put Um Loai's family in any danger. What if they do find out ... think, Mais, think! She clears her throat to get rid of the scratchiness in her voice. "Oh, well ... just around Ramallah ... umm ... I visit Birzeit University sometimes, and then some shopping in the souk ... or a theatre show ... nothing special, really." She hopes he buys it.

The man looks her squarely in the eye, leans over her chair, Maisoon can smell the tobacco on his breath and the sour smell of his body. She tries to avoid breathing him in.

"Beseder. You're getting off easy this time," he steps back, allowing just enough space for Maisoon to pass.

She is halfway to the door when his booming voice stops her. "And don't think that I'm so stupid as to believe you. It's just your lucky day today! Next time I catch you here, you'll be reciting names to me, understood?"

Keeping her posture straight, she walks to the car in a direct line. One foot in front of the other. She sits behind the wheel, turns the key in and drives slowly past the soldiers, making sure to keep her eyes on the distant horizon. She stops the car on the side of the dirt road to wait for the blonde woman. She didn't even tell me her name. A white Subaru stops next to her. The old man with the dried-up river tracks on his forehead rolls down his window to ask if she needs any help.

Seeing the distress in her eyes, he changes his mind and instead one of the veiled women says, "Don't let it in, binti. That's exactly what they want. For your body to make room for it. Go home, take a shower and clean yourself from their dirt."

When the blonde woman finally emerges from the gate, Maisoon can see that all vitality has been squeezed out of her body like the juice squeezed out of an orange. She collapses into the front seat, pushes the flip flops off her feet and puts her feet up on the seat. Her chin resting on her knees, she stares ahead.

"So, I'm headed to Haifa. That's where I live. Where do you want me to drop you off?" Silence. "Oh, I completely forgot. I'm Maisoon." Silence.

Ten minutes of silence passes.

Then, as if she remembers, "Christina. But everybody calls me Chris ... they took everything ... all of my work, and my equipment ..."

Maisoon can't imagine how she'd feel if her jewellery sketches were taken from her. "So, Chris. Is there any specific place you want me to drop you off at?" She tries to sound casual.

"Well, actually ... I don't know ... I've got a few days before I have to be back ... I'm with friends ... I don't know ... I don't have a plan really."

"Aha ... so how about staying in Haifa for a few days until you figure out a plan?"

"Yes ... I could do that ..." Chris replies absentmindedly. She half climbs into the back seat to grab something from her backpack. She fishes out a sketchpad and some stubs of oil panda colours—the soldiers didn't think them significant enough to confiscate—and begins drawing at a furious speed.

Maisoon remains silent behind the wheel, stealing short glances at the pad. A line of saber marking the boundaries of a village, some crude hills, and even cruder houses. A few mosques sprinkled through. Very pastoral and surreal—hiding the fact that this village, as many others, sits on only small parts of its original land. The saber have long been confiscated. How much do you know, foreigner, of the sadness of these hills? The scenery is slowly changing; they are leaving the scattered villages and hills to the darkening day. Swimming towards them are the monster oil refineries and chemical plants on the northern boundary of Haifa.

"So ... since you don't have any plans, I'm taking you home for some nice hot tea. It's getting late. You can stay at my place for a couple of nights," Maisoon says as Chris offers her a cigarette.

"Oh, you really don't have to do that ... I mean you've already done so much for me," Chris closes her sketchpad.

"No, I don't have to. And I really wouldn't if I didn't want to ..." Maisoon inhales the poison of her cigarette deep into her lungs.

حيفا فراجمنتس

In her kitchen, Maisoon has her back to Christina, preparing two glasses of na'ana shai when she feels the warmth of the other woman's body. Two hesitating hands slowly draw a pattern on her back. The hands are on fire. Maisoon's back arches, she closes her eyes and imagines Shahd's hands on her back. Then her whole body recoils, Christina withdraws to her chair and picks up her book.

The water boils. Green leaves of na'ana slowly swirl in the clear water. They sit at the kitchen table in silence. Christina continues to read her book. Maisoon is thinking of Ziyad—he is on his way to pick up his car. Christina puts the book down.

"I'm sorry, I don't know what just happened ..."

"It's all right," Maisoon's flat voice splits the sentence in half.

"No, it's not like that ... I ... it's just that ... my hands ... they just ... it was something deep in my stomach that made them reach for you. It wasn't my brain giving the orders. I really don't know what happened ... maybe all the stress from the checkpoint ..."

Silence followed, broken by the sipping of shai.

"I'm not angry," Maisoon's voice softens as she sees the distress in Christina's eyes. "It's this madness ... makes us do irrational things ... it's all right ... don't worry about it ..."

Now it is Christina's turn to shrink back. She gets up from the chair, "No, it's not all right. I ... I have to leave. I did something ... something that I shouldn't have ... to you ... and you're just too polite not to throw me out."

Maisoon reaches for Christina and hugs her, Christina's slight body almost fits inside hers. She holds her tight and soft. "Shhh ... it's okay now ... really ... go on ... you can cry ... just let it all spill out. All the dirt of those soldiers. Just empty your brain of all the ugly words they hurled at you today. You know you're not what they said you were."

Christina sobs into Maisoon's shoulder. Maisoon moves her hand up and down Christina's back. Softly.

Two strangers bound by first interrogations.

"What's a sharmuta?" Christina asks when they are seated again at the kitchen table, drinking the now lukewarm tea.

Maisoon's laughter chops the air around them.

حيفا فراجمنتس

Christina spent a week in the apartment above Um Muhammad's vegetable stall. On the first day, Maisoon took her to Wadi Salib, a neighbourhood with homes once belonging to Palestinians that had been confiscated under the Absentee Property Law after the establishment of the state of Israel. They walked in and out of houses emptied of all laughter.

Christina, feeling like an intruder, took pictures of the dilapidated walls and windows with a view to nowhere. "I'd like to come back here again with my sketchbook. There are histories within these walls."

As they walked on, Maisoon narrated Haifa's last battle, as she knew it from her grandmother. It was the personal story of one family, yet reflected the catastrophe of a whole people.

They returned the next day and with only the scraping of pencil against paper for conversation, they sat with their backs against the cold stone walls inside one of the houses and sketched the window from within the lifeless salu. The following day they went to a different house and sketched another window, this time from outside. It was a week of ritual —documenting windows, doors, walls, and stones. Pinning them down on paper. Each night, they made plans for the following day—the Baha'i Gardens, the sea, the Carmel mountain, Akka. Each morning, they relinquished their plans and in a silent pact went back to Wadi Salib. There was another door waiting to be drawn ... another window and another wall. They couldn't just abandon them for the bulldozers, which Maisoon knew would one day come.

Maisoon etched with pencil the moaning of Haneen into the walls, the sparks of the wedding that never was outside the window in the black sky, the cracks between the stones, unhealed scars, the mud, the dried-up blood of life unborn, the dust beneath her legs ... all those tomorrows that never were. It was a sketch of her grandmother's story, the story of all grandmothers, the home of all mothers. Into this one room she poured their laughter from before and also their grief from after and the blood of that death.

She stretched and looked over at Christina's sketch. It was the same room, the same window, the same sky but a completely different home. Not a home, just a bleak room—in shades of grey darker here lighter there but still only grey— life extinguished.

Christina shrugged at Maisoon's confused look, "I'm an outsider. This is not my place. I can't sketch it from within like you," she pointed at the chaotic sketch in Maisoon's hands.

حينها فراجمنتس

At the beginning of the following week, Maisoon has some finished pieces she needs to take to the boutique and asks Christina if she would like to join her. "We won't be long. After that we can go back to Wadi Salib if you want."

They take the Carmelit up to the Carmel, "the shortest underground in the world," Maisoon laughs as they get off several minutes later at the last stop. They spend about an hour at the boutique, and while Maisoon is busy rearranging the jewellery, Amalia and Christina talk—mainly Christina answering Amalia's questions about her experiences and first impressions of the West Bank. When they emerge from the boutique,

131

the sun is halfway up the sky. They walk the short distance to the bus station in silence.

"Let's take this bus, it goes a longer way, but you'll get to see some new parts of Haifa," Maisoon points at bus number 5. They get on and sit close to the back, Christina by the window.

The doors close and they begin to descend from the Carmel—a winding road connecting mountain and sea, called Derech Hayam in Hebrew—the Sea Road. As they descend the mountain, Christina notices that the houses become less grand, the streets are not as clean and proud. She imagines the residents from on high looking down in disdain at the lower parts of town—Hadar HaCarmel, Wadi Nisnas, Halisa, Kiryat Shprintsak, Kiryat Eliezer.

"So, this story your grandmother told you ... about what happened to her in 1948 ... did it make a change in how you see things today? I mean, did it have a significant effect on your life?"

"You know, I never thought about it like that. Of course it affected me but not in any particular way. I mean, I can't isolate this or another experience and point to a clear effect on my life. It's a package deal, you see. Every one of them adds to the ones before it. And what are we made of, if not our past?"

The bus continues down the winding road, and towards the end reaches a bus station with about seven or eight soldier-boys standing around. It stops for about a minute and a half—which seems too long to Christina, who is sitting at the window, only glass separating the men from her. Weapons always make her edgy, especially when slung over the shoulders of boys. One is smoking, letting failed rings of smoke out of his mouth. The other is standing talking to him, and at one point shoves his hand down his pants to adjust his penis and scratch around it. The machine gun sways slightly with his exertions. These guns aren't like the ones she's seen before on the streets of Haifa and the West Bank. They seem heavier, thicker. Or maybe they're the same and only look more threatening because she's sitting next to a Palestinian woman who crosses that forbidden line every now and then. What if one of them gets on the bus and decides to sit opposite her, the machine gun pointing in her direction? What if he hears Maisoon's accent or, worse even, what if he hears Maisoon saying something not to his liking? She sighs with relief when the bus takes off without any of the soldier-boys getting on. Then, a second sigh on account of her blonde hair and fair complexion.

A couple, one of them holding onto a shopping cart, gets off at the next station. An old man walks by, holding a transistor radio to his ear, the antenna sticking out. The bus continues. Now they cross a clear boundary, leaving Kiryat Shprintsak behind with its dilapidated, colourless houses and enter Wadi El-Jmal—Ein Hayam in Hebrew.

"The Arabic name means the Valley of Camels while the Hebrew means the Eye of the Sea." Maisoon's commentary picks up, "The Arabic name comes from the area being historically a resting point for camel convoys coming from the North—Akka and the Sham, on their way to Jaffa, Gaza and then Egypt."

The bus stops, a young Arab woman gets on with two small girls. Nobody gets off. Maisoon motions towards the mother, "Look how calm she is? It wasn't like this some years ago. I remember after a bombing of a bus that I used to take regularly, I … I couldn't get on a bus any more. Everybody was taking taxis." She lowered her voice. "I took a taxi once but never again. Two men sitting in the back were discussing the security situation and how Arabs are all traitors and can't be trusted. Anyway, right in the middle of this, my mobile rings. I panic. It is Tayseer's number. I hesitate before answering. Then I hit the green button and my 'aloo' comes out sounding very Arabic … like I wanted to provoke … I didn't let my fear or panic show. I will never forget the faces of the two men when they realized I was an Arab. The enemy, sitting right there with them in that crammed space. After that, for months I would walk everywhere. If I needed to go some place far, I'd ask my father or Tayseer to drive me, or I would borrow my father's car."

The architectural scenery is breathtaking. Christina concentrates on the old stone houses. Greenery gone wild. Other houses are newer, but built in ways that are reminders of the past.

"But you can't say this is how it was for every Palestinian after a bus had been bombed. This is how it was for me. And I still can't get into a taxi. But this woman—look at her. Maybe she took the bus the day after a bombing. Maybe she didn't. Maybe a relative of hers was on a bus that was bombed and it has taken her years to get over the panic, maybe she's forced herself to get on the bus every day and that's how she's gotten over it. This is how it is around here, this is how we live ..." Maisoon shrugs.

A few minutes later, they are out of the residential neighbourhoods and on the main Sea Road, passing the National Maritime Museum of Haifa—with two warships exhibited in front of it, an unnecessary reminder of wars. After that, they're in the 'business' sector of down-town—car agencies, falafel and shawarma places, metalwork workshops. All of this among scattered unoccupied houses, their owners expelled in 1948.

They get off the bus one stop before Kiryat Ha-Memshala—the Government district, with its ugly glass buildings and lawyers' offices that are fast encroaching on Wadi Salib until one day, no Wadi Salib will remain. It's a short walk to the souk. At least we're not at the very bottom of this mountain, Maisoon thinks as they walk up Mar Youhanna alley.

# 20

و While Maisoon and Christina had spent the week in Wadi Salib, Shahd had noticed a change in Qais; his playful antics were becoming hesitant. He didn't threaten her with his broom any more. Even his walk took on a different rhythm. But when she saw him playing football outside with some of the boys, it was the Qais she had always known—mischievous and full of energy. He was clearly distancing himself from her. Why?

On Friday evening, as she was preparing shai with na'ana for the whole family, someone knocked impatiently on the door. She recognized it as a child's knock—fast but not strong enough for an adult. Unthreatening. But urgent. Half a minute later, Shirin came running into the kitchen.

"Qais wants you at the clinic, like issa issa. Very important. Adel is waiting for you in the salu."

Her brain went into a panic and she froze. The water was boiling, na'ana stalks were laid out on the counter, washed.

Shirin spoke up, "Yalla, go change your clothes and run. I'll finish the shai." Still, she didn't move … "I know, Baba likes his with three spoons of sugar. No sugar for Mama."

She was running. Soldiers machine guns eviction bulldozers soldiers soldiers. Qais! She ran faster. Little Adel's skinny legs were trying to keep up with hers. "Every … thing … is … all right … habibi," she hissed between breaths, knowing that the words probably had the opposite effect on the little boy. She didn't have time to stop and gather him in her arms.

When they arrived, both breathless, Qais was waiting for them outside. The grin on his face was immediately replaced by worry when he saw Shahd and Adel coming to an abrupt halt in front of him, both out of breath.

"Where are they?"

"Where are who?" now they were both confused. Both looked at Adel. "What did you tell her, habibi?"

"I ... nothing ... I mean, I said exactly what you told me to. That it's important."

Seeing the fear in the boy's eyes, Qais got down on his knees and held him to his chest. Adel's body resisted at first, but then slowly gave in. Qais felt the brief trembling. "Shukran habibi for bringing her," he whispered into Adel's hair. "Yalla now run home, and salam to your mama!"

After Adel was gone, they remained standing outside in the darkness for a while. "I thought ..."

"Shhhh ... I know. I mean, I didn't ... I'm sorry. Really sorry. It didn't cross my mind." He took her hand in his, and gently pulled her towards the lit corridor. "Come."

She wanted to follow him. She trusted him. But ... A young, unmarried woman, led by a young, unmarried man by the hand—in the darkness—into an empty building. She knew Qais's intentions were pure, she also knew that he was imbued with a liberal, western education and that it hadn't even crossed his mind that such short moments could go on forever in the minds of people here.

He felt her hesitation and stopped. "I understand. All right. Let's just sit over there then." He motioned to a wooden bench in a well-lit spot of the yard. She shrugged her shoulders and walked beside him to the bench.

"I guess your father didn't talk to you ..." he said as they sat down side by side but not too close.

"About?" she asked hesitantly, but her mind was racing. Did he find a scholarship for her to study medicine? Or was Baba upset about her work in the clinic? Were they closing down Dar El-Amal? Or maybe, just maybe ...

"I'm really terrible at these things, Shahd." He was concentrating hard on the pattern he was making in the dirt with the tip of his shoe. "So I'll just go ahead and say it." He got up and faced Shahd, his hands buried deep in his pockets.

"I ... I love you, Shahd."

Her breath stopped as she listened to him.

"I fell in love with you the first time you came in here. And I knew you were the one for me when I saw the gentleness and purity of your heart. The way you make the kids laugh. And your stubbornness. And your fearlessness ... Shahd, every time I see you, I fall in love with you all over again."

"I ... I don't know ... what ... I mean ..."

"You don't need to say anything now. I will explain everything to you. I wanted to talk to you about my feelings, wanted to tell you that you are the moon for me ... but I was so shy. And I knew that things are not done this way here. So finally I took to the ancient tradition and went to talk to your father. I asked for your hand. And do you know what he did? He just laughed in my face. He said that my European education was all wrong and did I think I would have to buy him twenty-seven camels and thirteen goats to marry you? He shamed me, Shahd. He said that he wouldn't decide for his daughters. That his daughters had all the right to decide for themselves. I went home with my tail between my legs. I was so ashamed of myself. But now I realize that I deserved all his scorn. What was I thinking?"

"Qais, I ... my father didn't mention anything to me ..." she was conscious of the warmth coming from his body. She smiled shyly, her eyes lowered to the ground.

"Oh, your father is just so ... I mean, this is Abu Loai!" they both laughed, recovering a little of their ease with one another. "Anyway,"

Qais continued, with more courage, "this is what I wanted to tell you. I mean ... Shahd ... will you be shreeket hayati?"

Do I love you Qais you are asking? Yes, I have fallen in love with that purity that's inside of you. The selflessness with which you give up hours of sleep, the dignity you sweep the floors with. The light in your eyes and your love for the children of this mukhayyam, your courage to build Dar El-Amal. And your audacity to dream big. For this place, for the children, for tomorrow, for us. Will I be shreeket hayatak? Can't you see it every time you chase me around with the broom, every time you look my way, every time you tell me Sabah el-kheir and Masa'a el-kheir salam, the way you say my name ...

Just when he thought her silence meant a crushing no, she scooted over to him, and placed her hand on his knee, palm up. He smelt her hair as it brushed his chin. His hand closed on hers.

"Shreeket hayatak," she whispered into the night, and smiled.

She didn't know what it would mean to be his partner in life. As she walked back home, her mind teemed with questions. Shreeket hayati ... my life partner. Great! You are so stupid Shahd! What does this mean shreeket hayati ... will he now decide my life for me? She began to panic. He will take me away from Mama and Baba and Shirin and Ina'am. And the memory of Loai. I should have asked him about his plans for us—for me! Will I become a housewife or will he let me study to become a daktora. And what about Maisoon ...

Walking back into the salu, her father smiled, while her mother looked at her with curiosity. "Why didn't you tell me, Baba? You just let me run there like majnouny! You know what scenarios ran through my head!"

"What did you tell him, habibti?" her mother's voice followed her down the corridor until it was shut out by the bathroom door.

"She said yes, of course! Look how excited and angry she is," Abu Loai said and stroked Um Loai's hair. "Just let her be for now, Um Loai. It's not an easy decision and she needs to think over what this will mean for her, and ..."

"And for us, Abu Loai." She completed his sentence, moving shyly away from his strong yet gentle hand.

"Married for more than thirty-five years, and she still acts like I don't know every atom of her body. Like we just got engaged." Abu Loai stood up, stretched his big, muscular body, gathered the empty glasses of shai onto the tray and started towards the kitchen. "And it's what I love about you habibti."

As Shahd lay in bed, little Shirin's bony legs wrapped around hers, her warm breath on her neck, she resisted the questions pushing their way into the bedtime story she was whispering into her sister's ear. When Shirin's breath slowed, she wriggled herself out of her wrap and tiptoed into the kitchen where her mother was sitting in the dark, sipping a glass of shai. The moonlight fell on her face in stripes, hiding the tiredness, revealing only contentment and a sly smile.

"You knew, Mama," Shahd whispered, her eyes widening in surprise.

"Your mama knew long before Qais came to talk to your father, Asal. Come, sit with me for a while and I will tell you all about it."

When the water boiled, she refilled her mother's glass and poured a glass for herself. She drew a stool from under the table and sat on it. "Yalla, tell me, Mama."

Um Loai took a sip from her shai, resting one elbow on the table. She smiled at her daughter. "You're a grown woman, my sweet, sweet Asal. Qais is a good man, and you will make a good life together. But it doesn't come without any effort," she looked away, and Shahd noticed a glistening tear in her mother's eye. "When he came to ask for your hand, Baba insisted I stay in the room and hear out his plans for you. Baba knew he wouldn't be the one to decide, but he needed to be reassured nevertheless. He's seen the spark in your eyes when you talk about becoming a daktora."

Hearing this, Shahd raised her head, "Baba ...?" she leaned closer to her mother.

"So Baba asked him and Qais said that it was all up to you. You can stay in Tal E-Zeitun and make a home here. You can run Dar El-Amal

139

with him. Or ... he said that ... you could go to England so that you could study medicine there," the tear burst out from Um Loai's eye and ran down her left cheek. "He said that he didn't have any plans yet, as the plans will be made by the two of you. Together."

"Oh, Mama! But I myself don't know what I want. I don't ... this is really ..."

"Listen, habuba, you know," Um Loai smiled as she stroked Shahd's hair, "you don't have to decide this evening about your whole life. You can get married, stay a while, and see where life leads you. You can plan, but sometimes life has its own ways. Give yourself time—four, five months, maybe even a year. I'm sure that between the two of you you'll come up with the right solution for both of you."

# 21

"Mais! Where have you been? I've been looking for you all week.
I called Ziyad, Tayseer, even your parents! I have some news!"

"What is it? Something happened?" Maisoon could sense the
excitement in Shahd's voice.

"I'll tell you when I come. You're not going anywhere, are you?"

"Just get yourself to Haifa, Shahd. Yalla!"

حيفا فراجمنتس

"I can't believe it! So I will finally get to meet this brother of yours,
Salam?" Maisoon and Shahd are sitting on the diwan, while Christina
is out on the balkon reading a book.

"You must be excited about the wedding," Maisoon gently strokes
Shahd's hair. "What's the matter? Come on, give me a smile."

Shahd reaches for Maisoon's hand, and makes an effort at a smile.
"I know, it's just that ... things will be different between us after I'm
married."

Maisoon waves her hand in the air, "Psh! So that's what's worrying
that mind of yours." Then, in a more serious tone, she continues,
"Friendships take on different forms, you know. I'm sure ours is strong
enough to survive you getting married. We'll figure it out!"

Christina walks in from the balkon, interrupting their conversation.

"Now enough about this, we have a trip to plan!" Maisoon raises herself from the diwan and turns to Shahd. "So, is Christina invited to this big wedding?"

"Of course, you're welcome to join us too, Foreigner! And to meet my brother when he visits." But the next moment, as if remembering something, Shahd becomes silent.

"What now?" Maisoon asks.

"The day after tomorrow is Nakba Day," Shahd is swallowing the words slowly, like the dry earth drinking in the first rain of Tishreen Thani.

Maisoon does not attend any of the activities commemorating the Day of the Palestinian Catastrophe. She has never felt the need to mourn or anger collectively. The three women—two olive-coloured Palestinians from each side of the wall and a blonde foreigner—are silenced by Shahd's words. Maisoon is thinking of checkpoints, trying to remember if she's heard any news about closures. When Maisoon sees that Shahd is waiting for her reaction, she collects herself, "All right. Let's see if I can borrow Tayseer's car. Nothing will stop me from meeting this brother of yours." The next minute she is on the phone, trying to reach Tayseer.

"Baba, I need to talk to Tayseer. His phone is turned off. Do you know when he'll be home?"

"He's in the Naqab for the week. And how are you, habibti?"

She was silent for a few seconds, thinking. Ziyad wouldn't let her have the car for two days. She had no other alternative. "Baba, I need the car for … um … two days … maybe three."

"Of course, no problem. For two days? Where are you going?"

"Shahd's brother, Salam, is coming for a visit with his wife, from Italy. And they're having a big party for him."

"Shahd, yes. So when do you need the car? I want to fill up the gas and also check the air in the tyres before you go."

"Tomorrow," hoping he won't remember the date.

"Tomorrow," her father repeats. "Which means you'll be there on Nakba Day."

142

"Yes, I guess. But what does it matter?"

"Mais, you know it matters. There might be a closure, you can get stuck there for an extra day, or more. And what if you get stopped at the checkpoint?"

"Baba, all I want is to be there with Shahd and her family. I'm not planning on going to any demonstrations."

"You don't know what can happen." Majid's voice is rising now. "I don't want you to go there. Go next week. So you'll miss the big welcoming dinner."

Maisoon is silent, she wants to yell back at her father, though it isn't him that she is angry at.

"Mais? Are you there?"

"Baba. I'm sorry. I can't let the Occupation do this to us. I promised Shahd that I'll be there, and that's what I'm going to do." She holds her breath, waiting for her father's anger. But none comes.

She hears her father's low voice, "I'll have it ready for you by nine in the morning."

حيفا فراجمنتس

Christina and Shahd were in the car, waiting for Maisoon. Shahd's laughter came tumbling out of the open window. Maisoon smiled at her, savouring her friend's good mood. She wondered what Christina had said that made her laugh—but then, even a snail on the side of the road could make Shahd laugh. She got in behind the wheel, pulled up the seat, and adjusted the mirror to see Shahd's grinning face from the back seat.

"Yalla, we're on the road. Please fasten your seatbelts."

For a moment Maisoon felt annoyed that Shahd had decided to sit in the back with Christina, but she brushed away the thought. Christina was an easygoing woman and she herself had enjoyed her company for the last week. Besides, Christina had decided to try and stay in the mukhayyam and do some volunteer work. Shahd would probably be

143

seeing her around. They were now on the northern outskirts of Haifa, and Christina was already asleep. "So lucky that she can just put her head down—anywhere—and fall asleep immediately," Maisoon said in a low voice when she stopped the car to buy some cigarettes. When she came back, Shahd had moved to the front seat.

"I missed you, Mais."

"I missed you too, Asal," Maisoon unwrapped the pack of cigarettes, took one out and put it between her lips—unlit. She looked at Shahd.

"What? Why are you looking at me like that? Something wrong?" Shahd's smile faded.

Maisoon touched her fingers to Shahd's lips. Then she lit her cigarette and looked away. "Where do you get the strength to smile, Asal?" it was more a whisper than a question.

The smile snuck back onto Shahd's lips. "You know, I thought you'd never ask, Mais. Start the car, and I'll tell you."

It was Maisoon's turn to smile. She'd wanted to ask this question for so long, but feared to offend her friend. She fastened her seatbelt, put the car in first gear, pushed down the handbrake, put on the blinker, looked in the side mirror, and drove away from the kiosk.

Shahd waited until Maisoon finished her cigarette before she spoke. "Look, habibti. You're so obsessed with the past ... you have this need—I don't really understand it—to dig out the dirt from underneath your father's feet. And for what? So that you can go on? It's all an illusion, Mais! You claim you want to know your father. But he's not between the words. He's not in that dirt you're digging. He's sitting in the garden, smoking a cigarette. He's got white hair and he loves your mama. The Majid you're looking for is dead. He doesn't exist. And this Asmahan? Pshhh! Even her name is unreal. But you don't get it, do you? And Mais, until you let go of the paper Majid, you can't really get to know the Majid that is sitting in the garden."

Maisoon was becoming irritated, "I don't ... understand ... what's all this got to do with ..." In her agitation, she sped up and passed several cars.

144

"It has everything to do with where I get the strength to smile. Wasn't that your question? When we get to the neighbourhood, open your eyes really hard Mais and take a good look around. I recommend you start with Dar El-Amal. We want to live. And in order to live, we can't afford to wallow in the dust of history. We have to get busy and build something tangible. No, we haven't forgotten history but we go on. And you know what? If we ever lose our smiles and our laughter—then we lose our humanity. Christina asked me if we have hope. You know what I told her? That if we ever lose hope then there will be no reason for us to wake up in the morning."

Maisoon almost missed the dirt road leading to the hills, bypassing the checkpoint. She had to make a sharp turn right and the car swerved as it swept off the asphalt, jerking Christina in the back seat.

"What the fuck?!"

"Everything is fine, Chris. Just Mais here can never remember where to turn off so that we don't have to stand in that stupid line with those kids playing soldiers," Shahd turned around to face Christina, who was staring behind them at the cloud of dust. Then she turned to face Shahd with questioning eyes.

"Ok, so here's the plan. I talked to Mama about you, and she said she didn't want to hear anything about it!" Christina's eyes now widened. "She said that no family in the mukhayyam will host you if she doesn't," a smirk again. "So ... you'll be staying with us."

Christina reached over to Shahd and half hugged her, half hugged the back of the front seat. "Oh thank you thank you! Or, I mean ... shukran!" Then, she slightly punched Shahd's shoulder, "You had to keep it to yourself until now?"

"Well, of course! We needed some kind of a distraction when driving through the no-go area!"

All three women were laughing now. The car was bumpily making its way to the mukhayyam, alive with laughter.

They arrive at lunchtime and park the car in front of Dar El-Amal. Um Loai brings them a big pot of stuffed grape leaves, an Arabic fattoush salad, olives and pickles. They sit in Qais's office around a low round table, eating straight from the pot.

"You seem to get a ta'ashira real easy, Shahd, when some of the men I know have to wait for months," Qais is speaking with his mouth full, forgetting his English manners along with the fork.

Shahd stops chewing. Maisoon studies the curved shape of her pickle. Christina, sensing the tension, remains focused on her food. "So what's the secret, Shahd? Come on, you have some soldier friends? Or better yet, you know someone higher up?"

Shahd pushes the low table with her knees and stands up. She stares down at Qais, fingers curled digging into the flesh inside her palms. Qais stares back at her. Christina makes herself smaller by drawing her knees close to her body. Maisoon considers saying something, looks from Qais to Shahd, then back to Qais. No—the anger in his eyes isn't vicious. She's confused, but the urge to defend Shahd is receding. She sits back, her body relaxing, and watches them.

Qais stands up slowly, keeping up with Shahd's stare. "Come, we need to talk," he says in a calm voice, "just the two of us." He waits for her to lead the way. And she does—to the back yard, where she feels most at home.

They settle on a low stone bench right in front of the freshly dug-up dirt with the bulbs she planted a few days earlier. She picks up a handful of dirt and closes her fist over it.

"You're mad at me."

He takes her hands in his, taking some of the dirt and rubbing it into her palms. "And do you know why?"

"Because I put myself and Maisoon in danger when we take the back roads."

"You should know better than English me that even breathing in this place can be dangerous." He pats the loose dirt around one of the bulbs. "No, Asal. I'm not mad at you for that. In fact, I'm not angry at all. You make your own decisions. I'm just ... a bit saddened that you don't ... you know ... trust me."

146

She stops playing with the dirt in her palms and lets it fall back to the earth.

"Why are you surprised, Asal?"

"Because ... you ... never called me Asal ..." her voice comes soft and hesitating, but she is looking him straight in the eyes.

"But you are. That's the meaning of your name, isn't it? Shahd, Asal, honey. And that's what you are to me—sweet like asal." He is now smiling at the bulb. "But soon we will be one family—the two of us. And you know that we can't build anything solid without trust, Asal."

She stands up and faces him. This time, he stands up too, to be eye level with her. Their fingers touch. There is some dirt lodged underneath two of her short fingernails. "Trust."

"Why is it so difficult for you to get it into your head? Your father was right when he told me you had stones in there!"

"He said that?"

"Now don't change the subject, Asal."

She takes a step backwards, losing the touch of his fingers for a moment, and lets her hands drop to her sides. She looks at the stone building behind him. "Stones ..." Then she reaches for him, "Trust, you say. Tayyeb, let's try trust, Qais." She smiles and walks back inside.

Qais remains there a few more minutes, rubbing the dirt into his palms. As wild as she is on the outside, she is very fragile on the inside. But he can't be her anchor. He wants them to sail together. He turns back inside, with the knowledge that he has made the two most important decisions of his life—that of Dar El-Amal and Shahd.

حيفا فراجمنتس

After what Shahd had said in the car, Maisoon decided she would put Majid on pause—at least while in Tal E-Zeitun. Ever since she discovered his writings and the photographs, not a day passed without her reading his papers, looking through the photographs, thinking of him. Yes, Shahd was right—she had become obsessed with her father's history.

147

His love for Asmahan had become the mirror against which she held her love for Ziyad. Or Ziyad's love for her.

A deep feeling of contentment washed over her, and she decided to really enjoy her time in Tal E-Zeitun.

# 22

ع "I can't, Mais."

She's washing the dishes when the words land in the sink, splashing, sending angry droplets of soapy water to land on her arms. She blinks. The glass she is holding almost drops from her hand. She turns slowly to face the kitchen table. "Can you explain to me in simple Arabic what you mean by that?"

Ziyad is studying his palms, avoiding her eyes. "So you just expect us to drive into the village, and walk into my parents' house and I'm supposed to introduce you as what? My girlfriend from Haifa? The one I spend drugged-up nights with? The one whose body crawls into mine and sleeps there tucked inside twice a week?"

She is silent—her anger slowly gathering in the marrow of her bones. When she speaks, her voice remains calm. "Aha. I think I'm beginning to understand how it's supposed to work. But correct me if I'm mistaken. I'm the one whose life is pushed to its limits. And you get to keep yours all tidy and clean while you hide me from your parents so you don't have to deal with it. Right?"

Ziyad tilts his head to one side, "I'm sorry ... For Allah's sake, Mais, what's your problem? I want to marry you! I want us to be a real family. Just say yes and we'll drive to my parents' house right now and I'll introduce you to them and tell them we want to get engaged. Allah knows my mother will be so happy." As soon as he says the last sentence he regrets it.

"Your mother? So you just want this to please your mother? I don't want to get married, Ziyad! Get that through your thick head! I'm fine as we are right now. I don't need anything more out of this relationship." Maisoon drops onto the diwan.

Ziyad remains sitting at the kitchen table, his head between his hands. Several minutes pass in silence. Then Maisoon attacks again, "And what if I said yes? Do you think your family would accept a Christian, independent, city woman?"

Ziyad looks at her, not believing what he is hearing. "What? Maisoon, do you think that because my family is from a village and Muslim that they are backward people?" His anger is rising in his throat.

Maisoon doesn't look at him, and replies in a low voice, "Look what happened to Baba and Asmahan ..." the words come out of her without thinking.

"So this is what it's all about. I see. Your father and his Muslim Asmahan. A lost love story." Ziyad gets up, grabs his backpack and makes for the door. Before walking out, he looks back at Maisoon, "I'm really sorry that you can't just live your own life." The door slams behind him.

Left alone, Maisoon wonders why she finds it hard to commit to a serious relationship. Her line of defence has always been that she wants to stay independent and free. But now she's not so sure. Ziyad had tried to convince her it was all in her head—she couldn't believe him. It wasn't in her head. It was in every atom of her body. Lack of oxygen. Draining her. With his every touch, he would draw more air from her body. Every time he left, she'd send a message to his mobile:

"I can't breathe, I'm suffocating and need some private space."

Ziyad called it something else. For him, it was hesitation on her part. Indecisiveness about being with him. But he always let her have the several days of aloneness she requested. Until she disintegrated, giving way to her longing. It was a pattern they had both become addicted to. But his leaving now is different. It tastes final. I just want to crawl inside

150

your body and make a small corner for myself there. I want to stay there until all the air in the world runs out.

Is this how love is supposed to feel?

She is paying a heavy price for her own stubbornness of refusing a mahbas on her finger to remind her that she is owned and imprisoned by a man. But would it have been worth the price? Wouldn't Ziyad allow her the freedom she so worships? Maybe he would. But the very concept of him 'allowing' her, giving her permission, disturbs her. But it wasn't just that. If Ziyad were different, if he were more like Qais, with passion for a cause they both believed in ... maybe it would have been different then. As it was, they didn't have enough in common to build something of their own—not something with real substance to it.

دينا فراجمنتس

Asmahan                                                        أسمهان

when I'm with you in the bayader parts of me fall off
your body so tender that I'm afraid to touch you
lest your beauty diminish and—Asmahan

when you take the veil from your hair for me alone
I am. I become. I lust to cover my body with
your hair and feel its silky smoothness

I crave to worship you
kneel down and pray your love into me
to lose my self and find my self—inside you

terrified you will dissolve in my arms
intoxicated by the letters of your name in my blood
and one day I will be the ashes of your name

151

She put the poem back in the drawer, finding parts of herself in the young Majid.

It was intense love—physical, sensual. This part resembled what she had with Ziyad. But there was another dimension. Something all too familiar. She read the poem again—aloud this time, giving the words complete freedom to dance off chaotically. Then again, slower. Yours is not a love story only, Baba. She was beginning to identify a pattern—drawing thin parallel lines between herself and the paper Majid, Asmahan and Ziyad—in swirls and spirals, until it was all mixed up like an unsolved puzzle. Reading it again, stopping at the words *parts of me fall off*, and, at the very end, *I will be the ashes of your name*. The whole falling apart between her fingers again—so fragile! And back to fragments.

> Pieces chipping off, leaving us with missing parts of
> ourselves.

> Baba, I am made of you.
> Parts of me also fall away.

And then—at last—making the connection.

> It's this place, Baba. This place.
> There's something about this place that makes us fall apart …

ديفنا فراجمنتس

The sound of the durbakki reached Maisoon's bedroom along with the laughter of women. Late summer was the wedding season; at least two weddings every week. Finally giving up on sleep, she climbed out of bed and went to the salu. She tried to focus on a pair of unfinished earrings only to abandon them again. For several days now, a disturbing sentence was haunting her which she couldn't locate. She woke each morning with the words etched inside her mind like stone: *Moment of rage, forever of agony.* She knew it was something so terrible that a human mind couldn't even begin to understand the meaning. Then realization came to her in slow motion. It could only be one of her father's lines. She quickly took out the box containing the poems—she was sure it was from a poem—and spread them on the floor. She found a short fragment, dated 1982, on a single sheet of paper.

Petals of this child's soul crushed [no] mercy
[ ] eyes darkened for [ ]
The flower's leaves smothered [ ] nightfall

Manacles of this beast, fury in the heart
[ ] moment of rage, forever of agony


The Sabra and Shatilla massacre. For her, it was paper history. For her father, it was part of his very existence. Flashes of her distress during the Second Lebanon War back in 2006, when they all sat in front of the television and watched the rubble after each bombing, came back to her. Haifa had turned into a ghost town; many residents were leaving their homes, heading south to stay with friends and relatives. Cats were locked up inside for weeks with no food or water. Tayseer had broken in to their neighbour's house because he couldn't sleep at night listening to the desperate mewing of their cat. For two weeks, the little black fur ball never left his side until that day when even the cat realized death had reached the centre of Wadi Nisnas.

They wake to the sound of missiles and go to bed to the sounds of Israeli airplanes over their heads and reverberations from Israeli tanks firing into the night, across the Lebanese border. Their existence is made up of shuffling back and forth between the living room, kitchen and bedrooms. They don't have the luxury of a shelter, as most of the buildings in the Wad are old, built long before anyone could think far ahead into the future to imagine the need for such commodities. Unlike the Arab villages, they can at least hear the sirens—though it isn't much help, only increasing their panic.

It is all surreal to Maisoon until the day a missile hits three houses away from her parents' home. Going stir-crazy, she had gone for a walk. The sirens go off as she is on her way back from downtown in a half-deserted street. For a moment she freezes, not knowing what to do or where to hide. The first muted sounds of missiles falling in the sea reach her ears and she feels an easing of her panic. Then an arm grabs her from behind and begins dragging her to a nearby building. She doesn't resist. And then it happens. One, two, three missiles—not muted but in full force, the sounds so close she feels the ground under her reacting violently. The silence that comes afterwards is numbing. Then panic. Looking in the direction of the smoke, she knows it is in Wadi Nisnas. Running towards home, terror rises in her throat, she tries to dial her father's mobile, quickly discovering she can't run and dial the number at the same time. Stopping, she scans the names stored in her mobile, but she can't remember her father's name. When it comes back to her she dials, the phone rings, no answer. She dials again, this time the phone is dead. Stay calm, the phone lines probably collapsed. She runs and runs, her body aching, her mouth open, gasping for breath. When she finally reaches Wadi Nisnas, she is floating along waves of horror and fear, increasing with the smoke that is only getting thicker. No, it can't be. Mama and Baba are inside the house, waiting for me to come back home. She runs into the street and in the short space of her walk it has changed. People scramble around a house as it collapses, screaming loudly, asking if there are any survivors trapped. It is Abu Ashraf's house that has been hit. The firefighters and ambulances haven't yet arrived.

She runs toward her parents' house. The house is empty. Her mother, never losing her logical thinking, has left her a note on the kitchen table "I'm with Um Ashraf. Father is helping the men and women outside. I hope Tayseer is ok. Couldn't reach him. Let me know."

154

Maisoon grabs the phone and settles in the garden. The phone lines are still down, so she dials Tayseer's number every thirty seconds. In between dialling, she notices the empty cat dish, dashes inside and comes back with an open tuna can, hoping that the cat will be tempted by the smell. The cat has become part of their family for these past weeks, and it is Layla who has insisted on giving him a name, even if temporary—Misho.

She can't turn on the television for fear she'll recognize the remains of the other hit buildings. She knows there are at least two additional locations where death has struck today. She keeps dialling her brother's number. With the phone pressed to her ear she hears someone behind her. She turns but for a moment doesn't recognize the man with the blackened face. He holds out his arms and she flings her arms around her little brother. Clinging onto each other they both start crying. After some time they loosen their arms and Maisoon whispers "Tayseer, Misho's gone."

Misho never returned after that day. Abu Ashraf's house was rebuilt, with fewer occupants to fill it. Today, the brand new house stands as a reminder—an alien among the old homes built a lifetime ago.

As always though, there is a hierarchy of suffering, and Maisoon was soon put to shame by the image of a Lebanese mother carrying blankets from a wreckage that was once her home, her five barefoot children shuffling behind her with hollow eyes. On Maisoon's mother's request, she had prepared an emergency backpack with the most important things: her passport and other documents, cash, a change of clothes, a few family photos and her laptop. The contrast between her choice to stay or leave and that of the desperate scrambling of the Lebanese woman made the pain she'd felt that day seem hardly legitimate in comparison.

# 23

ﭐ "Maisoon? Do you have any plans for the evening?" Amalia was studying a new ring Maisoon had just finished. "I thought maybe you could stay after we close up. There's something I want to talk to you about."

"Sure, I don't have any plans anyway." What could it be? She looked up from her work and watched Amalia hold the ring up to the light. The two of them—worlds apart—had settled into a comfortable friendship. Each respected the other's personal history.

At quarter to six, Amalia closed the monthly financial report and shut down the computer. Maisoon was sweeping the floor to the soft music of Mais Shalash. "Coffee?" Amalia asked.

"Yes, thanks."

They sat opposite each other at the counter. Amalia sipped her coffee with a serious expression on her face while Maisoon waited in silence.

"You know, Maisoon, you've become like a daughter to me, ironic as it may sound. Anyway, there's something I need to tell you. The first time you invited me to your parents' house, I was scared. I've never been to an Arab's—sorry—a Palestinian's home before. I was taught by my mother to hate Arabs. They were the enemy who wanted to destroy us. I know now that I can tell you these things, because you have the capacity to forgive.

"When you told me that you were Palestinian, I didn't understand what you meant. They taught us that those who remained in Israel after 1948 were Israeli Arabs. Not Palestinians. But you taught me that there are other narratives to history. At first I didn't want to listen to you, because you undermined all the values I carried. And you changed my history by telling me yours. But something inside me kept telling me to listen to you. And I'm glad I did.

"Why am I telling you all this now? Maisoon, from the moment I set my eyes on that necklace you were wearing the day I met you, I knew the hands that made it belonged to a remarkably talented artist." She paused and lit a cigarette before continuing. "I'll make it short. I would be very happy if you agreed to become my partner in the boutique. Not an employee or the in-house designer, but a real partner in everything."

Maisoon choked, struggled for a breath, searched for words, and failed.

"Everything is settled. I've talked to my lawyer. All you have to do is sign the papers."

Maisoon stared at Amalia, "I ... I don't know what to say ..."

"Of course you don't need to give me an answer right now."

"Amalia," Maisoon reached across the table and grasped Amalia's hand, "You know this means the world to me, but ... you have to understand something ... I mean ... even if you don't understand, you have to respect what I want."

"Remember how quiet and bland it was when you first came here? It was like a tomb—so boring! Look at it now—look at the colours, it's so warm and pleasant. You know, I didn't tell you this, but a few months before you came, I was about to close down the whole thing. I wasn't selling. And then you came."

Maisoon looked around her, and for the first time she saw that the boutique looked just like she would want her own place to look. It belonged to her as much as it did to Amalia. Her designs filled most of the shelves and showcases. She walked around the table towards the older woman and embraced her. "I love you, Amalia. And I'm really honoured. But I can't give you an answer right now. It's a big decision for me." She brushed a tear from her cheek.

"I know dear. Take your time. We're not in any hurry."

حيفا فراجمنتس

"Amalia wants me to become her partner in the boutique." Maisoon was sitting with Layla in the garden, enjoying the cool afternoon.

Layla looked up from the book she was reading, a smile spreading on her face.

"But I'm not sure about it, Mama. I mean, she's a Yahudiyya after all."

"Now wait, habibti. What did you tell her?"

"My first instinct was to decline. But then I told her I needed time to think about it. I don't want to make such a big decision in a hurry."

"Make what decision, Mais?" Majid asked as he walked out with the shai.

"Maisoon just got a partnership offer from Amalia," Layla said.

"I see," Majid frowned as he put the tray down and looked at his daughter.

"And what do you think about it Layla?"

"You know what I think, Abu Tayseer. I think she should go with her heart."

Layla turned to Maisoon, "But of course it's your decision. I'm glad you came to us to hear what we think, but ultimately you're the one who has to decide."

Maisoon fidgeted in her seat, aware of her father's gaze on her. Layla knew what Majid's silence meant, and she got up with her book. "It's getting too dark to read outside," and left them alone.

They sat in silence for as long as it took them both to smoke a cigarette.

"So, what do you think Mais? Why the hesitation? Isn't it what you wanted all along? To have a business of your own and be independent?"

158

"It's not that simple. Is it Baba?"

"It's only as simple as you make it, Mais."

"But … it's complicated. She's … a Yahudiyya … and … it's just …"

Majid waved his hand. "Now listen to me Mais, and listen carefully. I'm going to tell you the last part of my story, the part that hurts the most. And then you decide for yourself. I know you wanted to know why I eventually studied economics and never pursued my dream of becoming a playwright. You see, I wanted it so badly, but I was a fool and an idealist. The local theatre scene was still so limited back then, and I saw my friends whose works were played in local theatres, but not beyond. The fact that we were disconnected from the rest of the Arab world didn't allow local artists to break through the barriers of the local scene. Yes, of course some made it. But they were the exceptions, because they were truly great. Maybe it was fear that I wouldn't be good enough that stopped me. There were other options to consider, of course—assimilate into Israeli society and write plays for the Israeli public, but that was never an option for me. Or I could have left this place and pursued a career abroad, somewhere in Europe. But that wasn't an option for me either. Looking back, I think I was a coward. Only cowards retreat without trying. I could have written plays locally. But since I opted out, I will never know what might have happened."

There was sadness in Majid's voice, but the olive branch on his forehead was slowly unfurling, replaced by a virgin plant with shallow wrinkles. "Life is about change, Maisoon. And every fork takes you on a different path. I know you're thinking about the fact that Amalia is Yahudiyya, and how that will affect your friendship with Shahd and how Um Loai will look at you, and how, if you become a famous jewellery designer, what people will think about you having a Yahudiyya partner. But remember also what I told you. They have their own battles and we have ours. I agree with your mother. Follow your heart. You've been doing it for years now, and been so good at it— quitting medical school, going out with this Ziyad of yours, refusing to get married. I think you're a brave young woman, Maisoon. And if you look back at these decisions, they were all made with your heart. I'm sure you don't regret any of them. So, just go home, take your time, and make sure you listen to what your heart is telling you. And don't forget that your world is so much different from what mine was all those years ago. Things change."

Maisoon listened to her father in silence, and when he finished speaking, she tucked a wild sliver of hair behind her ear, got up from the chair, and hugged her father from behind. It was a slow hug, touching her cheek to his unshaven one, moving her head down to his neck, finally nestling in on his shoulder. "Thank you, Baba. I needed to hear this from you." When she looked up, she saw Layla standing at the kitchen window, smiling.

Walking home, her mind buzzed. Shahd would understand, she knew this. But what about Um Loai, would she understand? Majid was right. But only partly. They were different, but also the same in so many ways. United by tradition, history, language, heritage. Divided by Occupation. There was always this pull, this tension between the here and the there. But she belonged here, in Haifa. And there was a reality here. Two peoples, sharing the same spaces, bound by history. So much was ruined, so much pain caused. But she knew she didn't have to compromise her art—she could continue making designs with Palestinian history, become a partner with Amalia, and yet stay true to herself. By the time she reached her home, she had made up her mind. She would embrace the more difficult choice.

# 24

Maisoon lifts her hair off her neck; it's a small relief from the heat. She pushes her chair back and leaves her worktable. On the diwan she goes through her father's history and finds the letter of the doors. Scanning down the lines, she finds where she'd last stopped reading.

These doors—I look at them now from their other side, the rain-washed wind-cracked side. I touch the cracks running from top to bottom. They hold the smell of mother's kusa mahshi and wara'a dawaly. She would come here in the morning when I was just a small boy and would sit on the tiles with her feet crossed under her long abaya. In her apron was the wara'a dawaly and in front of her the tushut with the rice specked with meat. I would sit with her and try to help but my hands were never good at rolling the wara'a into the neatly packed rolls. So I just sat there with my kurras and practised my *alef ba ta'a geem ha'a*. Mother would look up every few rolls and smile at the way I drew the letters. She said I never wrote. I only drew the letters. I was fascinated how the shape of the *meem* changes from the beginning to the middle to the end of the word and even when it's in the middle, it changes according to the letter coming right before it. So does the *ha'a* and the *geem* and the *noon* and the *kaf*. How I love the written letters of this language. I wish I could paint: I would paint the letters into beautiful paintings.

One day I was sitting on the tiles (I was maybe six years old) and mother came home smiling with something big bulging out of her bag, the shape of a picture frame. She sat down next to me and looked me in the eyes and her smile was suddenly gone and I became scared. I thought something bad had happened because it was a very serious face she made. Then out of her bag she took a very thick book. You see Asmahan I was already reading but father never brought me any books even though he studied in Dimashk and held an important position. So mother gave me this book and and then apologized: "Majid habibi I saw this book in the maktaba," and she lowered her eyes to the tiles, "but your mama can't read and I couldn't ask the bookseller what is inside or even what is the name of it because ..." and she fell silent, and I was silent because although I didn't really understand, I felt her shame. I took the book from her and I read the cover *Alf Leila w Leila.* Then mother smiled broadly. She was happy she hadn't bought me something boring or something that only grown-ups could read. But I saw the sadness in her smile. "Mama, we can read it together. Here, on the balkon. Every day after lunch—just you and me Mama. Every day, just one story." She was happy and I was happy and the next day we read together.

I am sending you this letter with Mahmoud knowing it may not reach you so I am making a copy to keep for you just in case. In case what—in case I see your face again?

Maisoon's stomach growls, she hasn't eaten since morning. She gets up from the diwan and walks through the long narrow corridor that connects the diwan with the kitchen and her bedroom. She walks into the kitchen, opens the fridge. Closes the fridge. Retraces her steps back to the corridor—and there they are. The two light-blue doors, even more cracked than in Majid's writing. She has never given this corridor much thought, passing through it from one side to the other. She was vaguely aware of the doors; when she first moved in she tried to open the windows but discovered the bars were on the wrong side and

162

laughed at the stupidity of the person who had installed them.

She now stands in front of the doors, her hand reaching for them. She touches their wrinkles, her finger going deep into the wood—it's rough, the creases curving downwards. She pulls at the door handles but then sees the thick iron lock holding them prisoners. The key. There was a key. Baba gave it to me. Where did I put it. The kitchen. She returns to the kitchen and opens a drawer where she keeps all kinds of useless small objects—wine bottle corks, seashells, small pebbles, tin cans, and yes, there they are—two keys, one medium sized and rusty, with four teeth; the other smaller, less rusty. They are bound together with a piece of black thread fraying at the ends. She hurries back to the corridor and stops in front of the doors. Peeps through the dirty windows, how come I never thought of cleaning you two? She feels the roughness of the tiles under her bare feet—still the original ones. She turns to face the far end of the corridor, the door to her apartment, with the diwan two steps along the wall. Then the bathroom, her bedroom, and the kitchen at the end. The light-blue doors are the only doors on this side of the wall. I need to do something about you, give you back some life. The paint on both sides of the walls is coming off, ugly patches of grey and brownish yellow underneath. Mould has gathered in the upper corners where the walls meet. She smells the mustiness.

She takes in a deep breath and, with a shaky hand, inserts the key into the lock. It resists a little, metal scratching against metal, before turning. The lock snaps open. She hesitates, will you croak as with Baba or will you extend me a silent opening like sitti Widad? She slowly separates the doors. They open not with croaking, but with screeching, Maisoon winces. Her eyes fall on a trunk in the corner of the balkon, its wood full of the intricate designs of woodworms. She bends down and smells its rottenness.

When she opens it, she half expects to find her grandmother's objects along with Majid's leather notebook. But all it contains is a thick net of cobwebs dotted with dead insects. She lowers the lid again and pushes it with her foot further into the corner of the balkon, asfi, teeta. She sits on the tiles and tucks her feet under. Holding on to the bars she looks into the remnants of a garden.

This whole time, Baba ... you were so close ...

# 25

Maisoon feels Shahd walking inside her mind at night. Mocking her for staying behind in all this mess. She misses her but she's happy for Shahd, believing things will turn out right for her and Qais. He is considerate, guiding their lives in the direction Shahd wants but is hesitant to articulate in a decisive way. She follows them from a distance, through Facebook and emails. Shahd has started her first semester in medical school, while Qais handles all the administrative and financial issues of Dar El-Amal long-distance. They are planning to come back to Tal E-Zeitun during Shahd's semester break.

Ziyad is also gone, she hasn't heard from him since their heated argument. She isn't sure if it's over between them. Two wholly and completely different worlds, with no overlapping. She walks in the rain, splashing through the puddles while he avoids even the raindrops. Her biggest fear was that he would try to tame her. Unaware that it was her wildness he loved most about her.

ﺣﯿﻔﺎ ﻓﺮاﺟﻤﻨﺘﺲ

"You put those boxes of Baba's writings up in my closet, didn't you, Mama?" her voice was steady. She needed to know.

"Yes, habibti." Layla didn't look up to face her daughter. "I didn't want you to discover it after … I mean, I wanted to give you a chance to know the Majid I fell in love with. It tears my heart apart to think that you only know this submissive man. Because he wasn't always like this ..." Her voice turned into a whisper. "He gave me the box a year after we got married. That was it. We never talked about it. I read and reread the letters many times, trying to piece his story together."

They were silent, sipping their kahwa.

"Maisoon, there's one more." Layla took a brown dog-eared envelope out of her bag, and placed it on the table in front of her finjan. "It's the only one about me." She gave Maisoon a sad but contented smile.

After Layla left, Maisoon took the envelope out to the balkon with a cigarette and a glass of wine. She had a feeling she'd need something warm in her blood. *A piece about Layla.* She began reading.

Asmahan, I try to burn my memories. But Asmahan doesn't give in; she keeps lurking in a dusty corner of my memory. Bits and pieces of her struggle to surge from underneath the surface; to breathe the breath of the present.

I know that Asmahan is the past. For there is another woman in my life now—Layla.

It was not love then.
It is not love now.
Asmahan used to walk in me.
Now I walk inside Layla's body.
I don't know how I walk her body.
But I do remember the way Asmahan used to walk my body.

I would feel her, pacing slowly back and forth, up and down, never resting. The worst would come at night, when she would move stealthily into my brain and walk there, not letting me sleep.

Love is a strange being. It is pure, it is wicked, it is dark and it is voluptuous. It is seductive and it is deadly.

166

And when love has said her last words, her words of night-time dreams, you are left only with memories. Memories that gnaw at your mind … your sanity.

I was willing to give up my everything for your love, Asmahan, but now I am left with nothing, and still I am a prisoner. A prisoner of memories.

I lost myself inside you, Asmahan … with your body tangled inside mine; my mind thinking your thoughts; my body feeling your heat your fire your weakness your pain the desert of your emotions. Cold!

*Layla*                                                         ليلى

Layla is my malak. She carries my weaknesses for me so I can be strong. She contains my pain … creating unknown dimensions of sadness for me to walk through. She takes away my madness, hides it.

Asmahan filled my world my body. Layla turned my body into a desert. But this desert bears the beautiful purple, thorny wildflowers of this land.

Asmahan was the Haifa bay. I was a drop of water, a grain of dry sand longing to be saturated to be filled with her waters. Layla is my land under which my roots grow.

It was love then.
It is love now.

حيفا فراجمنتس

The glue that makes it all stick, though in some illogical, twisted way. She drops the cigarette into the empty wine glass and stares at Um Tawfiq's laundry. At first, she doesn't notice any difference. Then Abu Nidal's strong voice calling a passer-by drops her back into the present. She stares at Um Tawfiq's socks, swaying haphazardly, facing different directions, the clothesline sprinkled with splashes of colour. Where are the sock-soldiers she's become so used to? Why aren't they marching in the wind today, all orderly and neat?

Her map of the man she imagined was her father is disintegrating, scattering in the naseem. The certainty of life in Wadi Nisnas, with its solidity of ancient stones is also dissipating. The comfort she draws from Um Tawfiq's sock-soldiers has been dislocated.

She stays there for a while, on her wicker chair, the sabra on the ledge of the balkon. The empty glass of wine with its drowned cigarette butt. The day is slowly waning, the souk gradually pushing its primary function of frantic buying into a corner to be replaced by a mix of socialising and relaxed shopping. Shahd and Qais are coming home in a few days' time. Christmas is less than a month away. She won't bring any guests this year. Tayseer has invited a special someone from East Al-Quds.

She slips Majid's last bit of history back into its envelope. A chime from the salu announces a message on her cell phone. She gets up, changes her mind, sits again and lights another cigarette. Ziyad? No, it can't be. She hasn't heard from him in over two months.

A last glance at the disorderly sock-soldiers. Where do I go from here? Which stepping stones do I choose? Which pieces of life do I pick up, and how do I put them together? She gets up, puts Majid's story in the drawer with the rest of his history, and picks up the phone to read the message:

"How about some red wine, a rock, a piece of the sea and the sky tonight?"

Smiling, she walks into the bathroom to take a cold shower.

# Naming conventions

*Abu Tayseer.* Father of Tayseer
*Um Loai.* Mother of Loai

This naming convention is used in Arab cultures to indicate that the person referred to is a parent. The name of the child is that of the oldest male son.

# Glossary

*abaya.* a robe-like dress
*ahlan wasahlan.* welcome
*Ajnabiyya.* Foreigner
*albi.* my heart
*alef ba ta'a geem ha'a.* Arabic ABC
*Alhamdulillah.* Praise be to God
*Al Quds.* Jerusalem (in Arabic)
*amar.* moon
*Aruset El-Bahar.* 'Bride of the sea', referring to Haifa; also 'mermaid'
*asal.* honey; it is the meaning of Shahd's name
*asfi.* sorry (feminine)
*Assalamu Alaikum.* Peace be upon you (Islamic greeting)
*balkon.* balcony
*bamiah.* okra
*bantaloon.* pants
*bayader.* fields or groves
*beseder.* all right (Hebrew)
*binti.* my daughter
*dabka.* Arabic traditional folk dance

*daktora.* doctor

*Dimashk.* Damascus (Arabic pronounciation)

*diwan.* low sitting area, composed of mattresses and pillows

*durbakki.* a type of drum

*Eid.* holiday, or festival; when used without a full name, it usually refers to 'Eid el Fiter'

*Eid el Fiter.* Feast of breaking the fast at the end of Ramadan

*Falasteeniyya.* Palestinian (Arabic pronunciation)

*fallaheen.* farmers

*finjan.* small-sized Arabic coffee cup

*gallabiyya.* traditional Arabic garment, worn by men

*Giveret.* Mrs (Hebrew)

*ha'a.* name of Arabic letter H

*habibi.* my dear (masculine)

*habibti.* my dear (feminine)

*habuba.* darling (colloquial)

*hajez/hawajiz.* checkpoint/checkpoints

*hayati.* my life (endearment)

*hazz sharki.* Middle Eastern shake (dance)

*ibni.* my son

*Inshallah.* God willing

*issa.* now; when repeated twice, it means 'right now'

*jhannam.* hell

*kaf.* name of Arabic letter K

*kafiyyah.* traditional Arabic scarf

*kahwa.* coffee

*kan ya ma kan.* once upon a time

*katyusha.* name of missile

*khalas.* enough (colloquial)

*khalti.* my aunt

*kohl.* ancient eye cosmetic, traditionally worn in the Middle East

*kurras.* notebook

*kusa mahshi.* filled zucchini

*laimoon.* lemon

*mabrouk.* congratulations

*mahbas.* wedding ring

*majnouny.* crazy

*maktaba.* library

*malak.* angel

*marhaba.* greetings

*Masa'a el-kheir.* Good evening

*Mashallah.* Praise God

*m'assal.* honeyed

*meem.* name of Arabic letter M

*mhammar.* Middle Eastern food

*min fadlak.* please (masculine)

*min shan Allah.* For God's sake

*muallem.* sir

*mukhabarat.* Arabic term for intelligence, locally referring to Shabak (Israel
Security Agency)

*mukhayyam.* camp; in the local context, it refers to refugee camps

*mumtaz.* excellent

*na'ana.* mint

*Nakba Day.* Day of the Palestinian Catastrophe, commemorated on 15 May

*nargila.* hookah

*naseem.* breeze

*noon.* name of Arabic letter N

*oud.* musical instrument, similar to the lute

*rajul.* man

*rakes.* dance

*rumman.* pomegranate

*Sabah el-kheir.* Good morning

*sabaya.* young women

*saber.* patience

*saber/sabra.* cacti/cactus

*sabiyya.* young woman

*sada.* plain

*salamat.* goodbyes

*salu.* living room

*shabab.* young men

*shaddi.* dice

*shai.* tea

*shakshooka.* omelette

*sharmuta.* whore (Arabic, but also used in Hebrew)

*shatwet Nisan.* April's rain

*shawarma.* popular Middle Eastern food made of meat

*sheib.* white/grey hair (of aging)

*shesh besh.* Turkish game, similar to Western backgammon

*shreeket hayati/hayatak.* my/your life partner (feminine)

*shu.* what

*shukran.* thank you

*sitti.* my grandmother

*souk.* market

*sumud.* Sumud means steadfastness or resilience, an ideology and a political strategy. It is the non-violent resistance, and the active decision of Palestinians to remain on their land, steadfast, despite all the injustices committed against them.

*ta'ali.* come (feminine)

*ta'ashira/ta'ashirat.* permit/permits

*Tammuz.* July

*tayyeb.* all right

*teen.* fig

*teeta.* grandmother (colloquial)

*tfaddali.* go ahead (feminine)

*Tishreen Thani.* November

*toda.* thank you (Hebrew)

*uzumi.* invitation

*Wadi Nisnas.* name of the Arab neighbourhood in Haifa

*walla.* colloquial, meaning 'seriously', used when someone is surprised, or as a question; literal meaning: 'by God'

*wara'a dawaly.* grape leaves

*yaba.* dad

*Yahudi.* Jewish (male) in Arabic

*Yahudiyya.* Jewish (female) in Arabic

*Yalla.* colloquial, meaning 'hurry up', 'come on'

*Ya rab.* Oh God

172

*Ya salam.* meaning 'Oh Peace', but used when someone is impressed or surprised by something

*yislam ideeki.* a term used to say thanks, literal meaning: 'bless your hands'

*zlam.* men

*If you would like to know more about Spinifex Press
write for a free catalogue or visit our website.*

### SPINIFEX PRESS
PO Box 212 North Melbourne
Victoria 3051 Australia
www.spinifexpress.com.au